Riding Shotgun to Denver

Cobb is an ex army major, cashiered for assaulting a fellow officer. He arrives in the town of Wentworth, where, after the death of a prison guard, he is obliged to escort some outlaws to gaol in Denver with just one man on his side.

But what should have been a routine operation suddenly becomes a dangerous mission as Cobb encounters storms and the mysterious Mr Smith. Smith holds a grudge against Cobb's charges and has vowed fatal revenge. Cobb, though, is determined to deliver his men safely, even if this means standing up to a foe intent on murder. From now on, his life would be on the line.

Riding Shotgun to Denver

FRANK FIELDS

A Black Horse Western

ROBERT HALE · LONDON

© Frank Fields 2001
First published in Great Britain 2001

ISBN 0 7090 6908 1

Robert Hale Limited
Clerkenwell House
Clerkenwell Green
London EC1R 0HT

Typeset by
Derek Doyle & Associates, Liverpool.
Printed and bound in Great Britain by
Antony Rowe Limited, Wiltshire.

ONE

It was with some relief that Cobb rode into the town in mid-afternoon. He was tired, hungry and felt very dirty. He had been travelling for almost two very hot and dusty weeks during which time the only sign of civilization he had come across had been an isolated farm two days earlier, where his reception had been far from friendly, even downright hostile.

The farmer and his woman had allowed him and his horse to quench their thirst and refill his canteen at their well but that apart, both the man and woman had made it plain that he and any other strangers were most unwelcome. He gathered that they had had an unfortunate experience with a passing stranger some years previously when the woman had been raped and what little money they had had been stolen. Since that time, understandably, they had treated all strangers as though they were not to be trusted.

They had refused him food even though he had offered to pay, maintaining that they had hardly enough for themselves, let alone passing strangers. All the time he had been there the man had kept him covered with a rifle and Cobb had no doubt that

he would have used it had he been given even half a
chance. He felt that he could probably have dealt
with the man had he needed to, but he decided that
it was not worth the bother. The one thing he had
gleaned was that some town called Wentworth was
about another two days' ride so he opted to keep on
riding.

Wentworth proved to be a town rather larger than
most, centred on cattle ranching and boasting two
saloons, two hotels, at least three rooming-houses, a
whorehouse, a good array of stores and a sheriff who
eyed him suspiciously. He was used to that and it did
not bother him too much. It seemed to him that
sheriffs of all Midwest towns made a habit of treating
strangers with suspicion. He supposed that it was all
part of the job.

The first thing he did was check into the nearest of
the rooming-houses, where he found that the accom-
modation consisted of a bunk in a dormitory and
that there were four other men staying, all apparently looking for work on the ranches. Cobb was not
looking for work, at least not as a ranch hand. In
truth he hardly knew which end of a cow was which.

He would have preferred a room to himself but he
knew that would have meant checking into one of
the hotels and he was not prepared to waste money
on what was, in his eyes, a luxury. At least the rooming-house appeared clean and was presided over by a
very large woman going under the incongruous
name of Rose Golightly. She was certainly no rose –
the kindest description of her would have been
'homely' – and her very size made it impossible for
her to go anywhere lightly.

She assured him that her place, at a charge of one dollar a night, was far superior to any rival establishment. He chose not to challenge her on this assertion and found himself a bunk just behind the door. He made a quick examination of the bunk and surprisingly, as far as he was concerned, did not find any unwelcome bedbugs. Bedbugs and rooming-houses usually went together in his experience.

There was a livery stable about a hundred yards down the street, where he stabled his horse, again at a charge of one dollar a night. He had serious doubts about leaving his precious saddle at the livery. Saddles were very expensive and in many places were prone to disappear if left unattended. Most travellers always kept their saddles with them. However, the livery owner assured him that the saddle would be perfectly safe, citing the fact that he was the brother of the sheriff as assurance. Cobb decided to take the chance even though he had known many dishonest sheriffs and their brothers. However, he was not prepared to risk leaving his rifle. Rifles too were very expensive and much sought after, especially a modern Winchester such as his.

His next call was to a barber's shop which advertised hot baths. He was not too surprised to be charged one dollar for the privilege. He began to wonder if anyone in Wentworth was capable of thinking in terms of anything other than one dollar, a feeling reinforced when he was directed to an eating house which also charged one dollar for a meal. He had eaten better food, but it was palatable and there was plenty of it and it was the first decent meal he had had for two weeks. His own cooking left a lot to be desired.

By the time he had bathed, shaved and eaten, the light was fading and the town's two saloons were beginning to come to life. Not having tasted alcohol for about a month, he decided to try the delights offered by the nearer of the two establishments, going under the name of Kate's Bar. Kate herself proved to be the sister of Rose Golightly and was almost as big. She, like her sister, appeared not to be a woman to be trifled with.

Cobb had to admit that she kept a very good beer along with a wide selection of whiskies and rums ranging from the locally made, throat-stripping moonshine, to genuine scotch whisky and good rum. After an initial beer, he followed it with a good scotch whisky even though it was far more expensive than American rye whiskey, but he felt like indulging himself.

The saloon slowly filled with thirsty customers and for some time Cobb was puzzled when they looked at him somewhat nervously, passing obvious comments amongst themselves, and seemed to deliberately avoid him. Although he was a stranger he did not think that as such he was anything unusual. Towns like Wentworth usually had a steady influx of strangers, most looking for work. It was not until he was approached by the sheriff that he discovered just what was wrong.

'Evenin' stranger,' said the sheriff. 'I saw you ride in just like I seen you take a bath at Jake's place.' He propped himself against the bar and took hold of a glass of beer which miraculously appeared. It seemed to Cobb that payment for the beer was also something of a miracle since he did not see any money pass over the counter. 'Now I like a man what makes a habit of takin' a bath when he comes into town,' continued the sheriff. 'To my mind it shows that he can't be all bad. Most the men round here seem to have somethin' of an aversion to soap an' water.'

'It's been almost four weeks since I was able to have a bath,' said Cobb. 'Last chance I had was back in some place called Cooper.'

'I've heard of it,' said the sheriff. 'I ain't never been there though. That's a long way an' across desert. What brings a man like you out this way?'

'Nothing really,' admitted Cobb. 'It just seemed a good idea at the time to head this way.'

'On the run from the law?' asked the sheriff, casually.

'On the run from an ex-wife and her brothers more like,' said Cobb with a dry laugh. 'No, Sheriff, I am not running from the law.'

'I guess runnin' from a woman is as good a reason as I've ever heard,' said the sheriff, nodding sagely. 'I sometimes wish I had the guts to take a runner from mine but I guess it's too late now. I must admit that I checked through all my wanted flyers as soon as you rode in but didn't find nothin'. That don't mean a thing though, I don't get to hear about some folk until after they've gone but I always check out any stranger against what I have. Sometimes I strike lucky but most times I don't, but I reckon most are wanted somewhere for somethin' or other.'

'A wise precaution,' said Cobb. 'In my case, though, you won't find any wanted posters with my name or face on them.'

'You checked in to Rose Golightly's place . . .' Cobb nodded. 'Yep, good place too, best roomin'-house in town I'd say. Not the cheapest but the best. The other two charge seventy-five cents a night but that also includes the bedbugs. Rose keeps a clean place, there ain't no denyin' that. Didn't she tell you about an ordinance we have here in Wentworth?' Cobb shook his head. 'She should've done,' continued the sheriff. 'I'll have to remind her to tell her guests. Yes, sir, here in Wentworth we have an ordinance about the carryin' of guns. No man is allowed to carry a gun within the town limits. Rose should have told you about that. Some folk have been gettin' kinda worried at you walkin' the streets carryin' a rifle as well as wearin' a handgun. They wanted to know just what I was goin' to do about it.'

'Your brother didn't mention it either,' said Cobb.

'Brother?' queried the sheriff. 'Oh, you mean little brother Jimmy. He owns the livery. Yeh, he should've told you as well I guess. The thing is, any man what don't obey the law is liable to spend a couple of nights in my jail, pay a fine of ten dollars, plus pay for any food he has an' then be kicked out of town. Thanks to that ordinance Wentworth ain't had no serious trouble in the last five years an' I intend to keep it that way if only because it makes life easier for me an' I'm all for the quiet life.'

'Well since nobody told me, how am I expected to obey the law?' said Cobb. 'Does this mean I have to spend a couple of nights in your jail?'

'Fortunately for you, the jail is full right now,' said the sheriff. 'That don't mean you can wear your gun an' carry that rifle though. It's on account of the scum I have in jail that folk are kind of jittery at the sight of you carryin' them guns. They have this idea that somebody might try to bust 'em out of jail.'

'They're that important, are they,' said Cobb. 'You don't have to worry, I'm not in the business of helping outlaws escape from jail. OK, so you have an ordinance about wearing guns in town, so just where do I leave them?' Cobb raised the rifle and looked at it. 'This piece cost a lot of money. You ought to know just how expensive Winchesters are. I don't intend to leave it where it might get stolen.'

'Yeh,' said the sheriff, 'I know that can be a problem. I usually take 'em an' keep 'em locked up safe until the owner either leaves town or finds work. If he finds work it's up to him where he keeps his guns, just so long as he don't bring 'em into town. So how long are you stoppin'? If it's work you're lookin' for I hear there's jobs goin' out at a couple of the ranches.'

'Looking after cattle is not my idea of work,' said Cobb.

'Well there ain't much else doin' round here,' said the sheriff. 'I guess that means you'll be movin' on.'

'I thought I'd give it a couple of days,' said Cobb. 'I need a break from wandering.'

'You don't look like your usual saddlebum,' said the sheriff, looking Cobb up and down. 'Besides, I ain't never met a saddlebum yet what heads for a bath as soon as he hits town. What's your name?'

'Cobb,' replied Cobb.

'Cobb,' said the sheriff. 'Don't you have any other handle to your name?'

'You can call me Mr Cobb if you like,' replied

Cobb. 'I've been known just as plain Cobb even before I left the army about five years ago. Cobb suits me just fine.'

'Then Cobb is fine by me,' said the sheriff. 'Yeh, you look like you was a soldier, I can tell by the way you hold yourself. I'd say you wasn't just a plain soldier either. We used to have a cavalry regiment stationed here some years ago an' they was more trouble than they was worth as far as I'm concerned. Lookin' at you an' listenin' to the way you talk an' the way you rode that horse, I'd say you was probably an officer. You talk like an educated man.'

'Very observant of you,' said Cobb with a smile. 'I was a major but not with the cavalry, I was in the Corps of Engineers.'

'Major!' said the sheriff. 'What made you give all that up?'

'I guess I just got tired of it all,' said Cobb. 'Well, maybe that's not strictly true. I was cashiered for hitting a fellow officer.'

'And did you?'

'Oh, sure,' said Cobb, this time with a broad grin. 'At the time it seemed a good idea, especially when I caught him and my wife in bed. I know it gave me a great deal of satisfaction at the time.'

'I wouldn't've thought they would cashier you for that,' said the sheriff.

'Normally they wouldn't,' said Cobb. 'The problem was that he and my wife denied it all and since there were no witnesses ... well, it was my word against the two of them. I suppose the fact that I hit her as well didn't help. That's when her brothers got involved and one of her brothers just happened to be my commanding officer.'

'I allus say that kin an' work just don't mix,' said the sheriff. 'I had my brother-in-law workin' for me as a deputy once an' that didn't work either. My wife reckoned I was too hard on him. OK, Cobb, I suggest we go along to my office an' you can hand over them guns. Some folk'll sleep easier in their beds if you do.'

'If that's the law, then who am I to argue?' said Cobb. 'Let's go. Do you want to take charge of my guns right now?'

'I'll take the Winchester,' said the sheriff.

Cobb felt the eyes watching him as he and the sheriff left the saloon and even before they had passed through the swing doors there was an eruption of chatter and speculation. They crossed the street to the office, which was almost directly opposite, and had to wait while a deputy on the inside unlocked the door.

'Can't be too careful,' said the sheriff. 'There's five men in there, all killers with more'n six thousand dollars on their heads.'

'How did you get hold of them?' asked Cobb as they went inside.

'Pure luck,' admitted the sheriff. 'They came into town four days ago an' like I allus do, I checked 'em against my Wanted posters. Two of 'em came up with fifteen hundred dollars each on their heads, so I reckoned the others was also wanted men and arrested 'em all.'

'You were taking a chance weren't you, five killers?'

'Guess so,' shrugged the sheriff. 'Didn't think

much of it at the time though. Me an' Ted here,' he
indicated his deputy, 'we just came up behind 'em in
Kate's Bar an' took 'em by surprise. It was easy. See,
they thought they was bein' very clever an' weren't
wearin' their guns on account of the ordinance.
Seems they didn't want to bring attention on themselves. When I wired Denver they told me about the
other three. The pity is I don't get to see one cent of
the reward money; all part of the job, they tell me.
I'm too old now, but if'n I was a younger man with no
woman to tie me down I'd take up bounty huntin'. It
sure pays a whole lot better'n a sheriff's salary. Six
thousand would set me up for life.'

'I suppose most people would be satisfied with that
much,' agreed Cobb. 'OK, Sheriff, here's my Colt
and my belt, you already have the Winchester. Do I
get a receipt?'

'You can have one if'n you want one,' grunted the
sheriff. 'Don't know what a piece of paper will prove
though. They'll be safe enough. I keep 'em in that
strongbox over there. Ain't nobody goin' to break
into that.'

Cobb examined the large, heavy-duty safe and
smiled.

'Give me ten minutes and I can have it open,' he
said. 'Part of my work in the Corps of Engineers was
breaking into things like this.'

'Just remind me not to leave him alone in here for
ten minutes,' said the sheriff to his deputy. He took
the guns, opened the safe and deposited them
inside. Cobb noted that there were several other
handguns and one rifle in the safe. 'OK Cobb, I
guess you ain't in breach of the law no more. You can

get back to you drink. Just let me know when you're
ready to leave.'

'What happens if you get trouble tonight?' asked
Cobb. 'With a full jail you have nowhere to lock
people up.'

'Then don't cause me no trouble,' said the sheriff.
'They'll be out of here in two days. There's a prison
wagon comin' in from Denver to take 'em to the state
pen. If there was only one of 'em somebody would
take him out to Scotswood an' then on to Denver by
the railroad. Five of 'em though is expectin' a bit too
much of any one man to handle. I can't spare
nobody to escort 'em an' I don't think I'd he able to
find any volunteers at any price.'

'You seem to be expecting somebody to try and
free them,' said Cobb. 'It seems to me that taking
them across country in a wagon is both slow and
inviting trouble.'

'My feelin's too,' agreed the sheriff. 'That ain't my
problem though. That's how Denver says they've got
to be taken an' I ain't about to argue. I just want 'em
out of here. What happens after that ain't my
concern. As for somebody tryin' to set 'em free, that's
only what they say. It's probably all just talk.'

'Are there any other strangers in town?' asked
Cobb.

'You're the first one since they rode in,' said the
sheriff. 'As far as I know there ain't nobody left town
in that time either, so there ain't no way nobody
could know about them bein' arrested. That's why I
say it's all talk on their part.'

'Well, as you say,' said Cobb. 'I suppose that once
they've been taken from your jail it's no concern of

yours. It certainly isn't any concern of mine either. Like you, I'm all for the quiet life. I think I'll have a couple more drinks and then turn in for the night. Good night to you, Sheriff.'

Cobb returned to Kate's Bar where, after a brief show of interest in him, everyone seemed to forget him and concentrated on other matters. He ordered another glass of beer and was approached by one of the girls employed by Kate.

'I'm glad to see the sheriff didn't lock you away,' she said, linking her arm through his. 'It makes a change to see a clean, decent-looking man. It wouldn't hurt for more men to take a bath a bit more often. I saw you go into Jake's earlier on.'

Cobb looked at the girl, who was probably half his age, and smiled. 'I must say that it makes a change for a girl in your business to look and smell nice too,' he said. 'Most girls I meet in bars think that all they have to do is hide the dirt with powder.'

'Kate makes sure we're all clean,' said the girl. 'I just wish she could he the same with some of the customers. Well, since we both seem to like the look of each other, what do you say about getting to know each other a little better?'

'How much?' asked Cobb. 'Even Kate wouldn't give it away for free.'

'Three dollars,' replied the girl.

'A mite expensive,' observed Cobb.

'Mister,' she said with a laugh. 'Like most things in life, you get what you pay for. I can assure you that three dollars spent on me is three dollars well spent.'

'OK,' agreed Cobb. 'Let's go.'

The girl, whose name, Cobb discovered, was

Maureen, led him up the stairs and along to a room at the rear of the building. 'There's six of us working here,' she explained. 'We live in these rooms where we're expected to carry out our business. The rooms at the front are for guests and Kate's own rooms. Even she does a little entertaining from time to time.'

'She's too big for my taste,' said Cobb.

'You'd think she was too big for any man,' said Maureen, 'but you'd be surprised at just how many men get turned on by her. Some men seem to like their women big, the bigger the better. Now, Mr . . . er . . . I didn't catch your name.' She slipped her arms around his neck and kissed him lightly on the cheek.

'That's because I didn't say,' he replied. 'Just call me Cobb.'

'Cobb!' she said, pulling away slightly. 'Is that all?'

'That's all,' he replied.

'You know, some men are really funny when it comes to names.' she said. 'The other night there was another stranger here who insisted I call him Smith, Nothing else, just Smith. Here you are, refusing to tell me your given name. Why is that? Why do some men seem to resent folk knowing what their given name is?'

'I can't speak for anyone else, but I've always been known as Cobb, even when I was in the army,' he replied.

'OK.' She shrugged as she pulled away and proceeded to unfasten her dress. 'Cobb you want to be, Cobb you shall be. I've a living to earn; I can't afford to waste time talking, unless that's all you want to do, talk. That happens from time to time as well, just like Smith. All he wanted to do was look at me and talk. I must admit that I didn't like the way he looked at me but he was paying so who was I to argue? Anyway, he had a gun and the way he fingered it I think he got more satisfaction from that than he would from any woman.'

'I thought men weren't allowed to carry guns in town,' said Cobb, removing his clothes and following her to the bed.

'They're not,' she said, lying down and stretching her arms up, inviting him to join her. 'That's the sheriff's business, not mine. I don't think he even knew he was in town. Anyway, he had other things to worry about that night, he arrested five other men. Something about them being outlaws, killers with big rewards out on them.'

'And this Smith was with them?'

'I wouldn't know,' she sighed. 'Are you more interested in him or me? Make your mind up, I could be losing business.'

'I'm intrigued about this man called Smith,' said Cobb as they dressed. 'The sheriff said there hadn't been any other strangers in town apart from the five he arrested. It seems to me he was wrong. Is he still around?'

'If he is, I certainly haven't seen him,' replied Maureen. 'I have the feeling that he left almost as soon as he'd finished with me.' She shivered slightly. 'The thought of him still sends shivers up my spine. Those eyes of his were very cold. Mind, it was the easiest three dollars I've ever earned, all he did was look at me and play with that gun of his. I sure wouldn't like to meet him in the dark though.'

'Maybe he was with these five men the sheriff arrested,' said Cobb. 'It seems strange that he should have turned up at the same time.'

'Mr Cobb,' she sighed. 'In my line of work it don't pay to wonder who the client is or where he's come from or where he's going. I don't ask no questions. What people do when they're not with me is no concern of mine. As long as they pay, I provide what they want.'

'Did you tell the sheriff?'

'What's to tell?' she said. 'He didn't do anything illegal.'

'Except carry a gun,' reminded Cobb.

'It ain't up to me to report him for that,' she said. 'That's what the sheriff is employed for. Now, Cobb, unless you want to pay another three dollars, your time is up. There could be other clients waiting downstairs.'

Cobb and Maureen returned to the bar where she very quickly found another client and returned upstairs. Cobb ordered another beer and, glass in hand, wandered round a few gaming tables, just watching, not playing. He suddenly became aware of the sheriff standing behind him.

'I just heard something very interesting,' Cobb said to the sheriff. 'It seems that while you were arresting those five men another stranger was being entertained by the girl called Maureen. It appears that he had a gun with him. She said his name was Smith.'

'That's a name which could apply to nine out of

ten strangers who pass through,' said the sheriff. 'It's usually either Smith, Jones or somethin' like Brown.'

'But I thought you said that those five were the only strangers through that day?'

'All five rode into town together,' said the sheriff. 'Neither me nor Ted saw anyone else.'

'But she was quite certain he was here,' said Cobb.

'Is he still here?' asked the sheriff.

'She hasn't seen him since.' admitted Cobb.

'Then if he ain't here I ain't goin' to worry about him,' said the sheriff.

'I suppose not,' said Cobb. 'It just struck me as strange, that's all.'

TWO

Apart from one of the other men in the rooming-house – who was the worse for drink – snoring loudly for about the first two hours, Cobb had a good night's sleep. For the first time in two weeks he had slept in a bed and really appreciated that fact. Although he had chosen the wandering life, he had never really come to terms with sleeping on the ground out in the open and had never learned how to cook properly; he had certainly not learned how to live off the land. His inability to cook meant that wherever possible he used eating-houses, which was why, shortly after dawn, he walked down the street to the eating-house he had used the previous night. His fellow guests at the rooming-house could not, according to them, afford such luxury. They used the stove provided by Rose Golightly to cook an unappetizing mess of pork and beans. Their cooking abilities appeared to be on a par with his and the pork smelled very ripe. He hoped that their digestive systems could cope.

The meal he had had the previous night had been adequate but nothing special. However, breakfast proved to be something else. There was a choice of a large steak – standard fare for any meal including breakfast in cattle country – or a thick slice of ham. Both were served with two fried eggs and fried hashed potatoes. Cobb opted for the ham. This was washed down with a large mug of coffee, all for one dollar.

After checking on his horse and, more important, his saddle, Cobb paid for another night, having decided to stay in town for at least two more days. He had no particular destination in mind and certainly no particular time in which to get there, and Wentworth appeared to be as good a place as any to spend a few days doing absolutely nothing. His only regret was that these days there were too many days spent doing nothing.

There were a few supplies he needed but there was no hurry to buy them and he spent some time wandering from store to store comparing quality and prices. Although he had money, he certainly did not have enough to throw around and had learned about being frugal if nothing else. He had the feeling that the prices on most items suddenly increased dramatically when he inquired. This feeling was reinforced when he met the bar girl, Maureen, as he came out of a general store.

'Good morning,' he greeted, raising his hat. 'What brings you out so early? I would have thought that a long sleep-in would have been the order of the day for you. You must work late.'

'Good morning, Mr Cobb,' she said with a broad smile. 'A girl has to eat, you know. Kate does not provide food, we have to see to that ourselves. If we leave it too late all the best has gone.'

'Prices seem pretty steep,' he observed. 'I asked about some beans and flour and they wanted to charge me twice as much as I usually pay.'

'I don't know how much you usually pay, Mr Cobb,' she said, 'but two pounds of beans and two pounds of flour should cost only fifty cents each.'

'I guess I must have a big sign above my head declaring I'm a mug,' he said. 'Maybe I should get you to do my shopping for me.'

'I think they try it on with all strangers,' she said. 'Have you found Mr Smith yet?'

'Mr Smith?' queried Cobb. 'Oh, yes, I see. No, I never even gave him another thought. Well, I won't detain you. Perhaps I'll see you tonight.'

'You know where to find me,' she said, laughing.

Although Cobb had not given any thought to the strange Mr Smith, the mention of him started him wondering again. Why he should bother was something of a mystery; after all, it really was no concern of his just who Smith really was or why he was apparently connected with the men in jail. However, for some reason he simply could not get the man out of his mind.

As he wandered down the street, he came across a group of eight men, including his four room-mates, lounging outside the offices of the Cattlemen's Association. As he approached, a large, well dressed man with a very arrogant air came out of the office and stood grandly on the boardwalk, obviously making certain that the men had to look up at him. He was, Cobb thought, a man who demanded to be looked up to. Immediately all the men gathered round hopefully.

'I've got two week's work for about nine men,' the man announced. 'Five dollars a week, all found.'

'Yes, sir,' chorused all the men at once.

The man looked around, counted all the men and turned to indicate another man dressed in everyday clothes who had just come out of the office.

'Give your names to my foreman,' he said. 'You can all start in the morning.' He looked about again. 'That's eight, I said nine.' His gaze fell upon Cobb. 'You!' he barked. 'Did you hear what I said?'

'I heard,' said Cobb.

'You're a stranger, do you want work or don't you?'

'Now that all depends on the type of work,' replied Cobb.

'Since when have the likes of you been able to pick and choose?' demanded the man. 'If you want work you'll take whatever's going.'

'If it's looking after cows, I'm not interested,' said Cobb.

'I see,' sneered the man. 'Cattle herding is too menial for you is it? You are indeed fortunate, sir, to have enough money to be so picky.'

'I get by,' said Cobb. 'And what money I have is my business but it was honestly come by.'

'I would seriously question that,' replied the man grandly, stretching himself to his full height and gazing down his nose at Cobb. 'You probably have never done an honest day's work in your life.'

'I'd say twenty odd years in the army was about as honest as they come,' said Cobb.

'That's even worse!' sneered the man. 'I've never yet met an ex-soldier who even knows the true meaning of work and most would steal the food out of your mouth given half a chance.'

'And I've never yet met a rancher who isn't out to make as much money out of those who work for him as he can and not think twice about grinding his workers into the dirt,' replied Cobb. 'Most are like you seem to be, rich enough to buy their way around. No, sir, I'm not interested in your kind of work.'

'Well I can assure you you will not find any other kind of work in Wentworth County,' the man sneered again.

'Then I'll just have to wait until something more suitable comes along,' said Cobb. 'I thank you for the offer,' he added sarcastically.

'Something more suitable!' exclaimed the man. 'Sir, I can assure you that as far as you are concerned nothing more suitable will ever come along. Since you have refused work, I'll make sure that nobody employs you, not even to clean out cesspits.'

'I don't clean out cesspits either,' said Cobb. He was beginning to enjoy goading the man. 'I'm sure you're more experienced at digging shit than I am.'

'Watch your tongue!' snarled the man. 'You are obviously unaware of just who I am. I can easily have you run out of town.'

'You can try,' invited Cobb. 'I hear this is a free country where a man can choose what kind of work he does, where he lives and how he lives. Good day to you, sir.' He raised his hat in a derisive manner, turned and walked away. He heard the man ask if anyone knew who he was. He did not hear if his room-mates said anything and he did not care. Later that day he was approached by the sheriff.

'I hear you've been upsettin' Lance Watson,' said

the sheriff. 'It don't do to get on the wrong side of Mr Watson.'

'And just who is Lance Watson, apart from obviously being a cattle rancher?' asked Cobb. 'He seemed to think he owned the place.'

'He does, as good as,' said the sheriff. 'Mr Lance Watson is the most powerful man in the territory and owns most of it. He even put up for governor last year.'

'He didn't get in though, did he? That ought to tell you something,' observed Cobb. 'I heard him ask if anyone knew who I was but I didn't think he'd get round to asking you.'

'He didn't so much ask who you was as tell me to make sure you leave town pretty damned quick,' said the sheriff. 'So I'm tellin' you.'

'OK, so you told me,' said Cobb with a broad grin.

'A word of advice, Cobb,' said the sheriff. 'In these parts when Lance Watson says somethin' everyone sits up an' takes notice, even me. I want you out of Wentworth by dawn tomorrow. You can collect your guns first thing in the mornin'.'

Cobb's initial reaction was to tell the sheriff to go to hell, but he decided not to bother. He had intended to leave the day after anyway and he was not looking for trouble. He shrugged but said nothing and decided that he might as well buy the supplies he needed. Remembering that Maureen had indicated that the prices he was being given were more or less double the actual price, he eventually succeeded in buying all he needed at a price he considered fair.

Later that afternoon a large wagon looking more like a cage on wheels arrived. This was the prison wagon the sheriff had mentioned. There were two quite elderly looking men with the wagon, both armed. It was noticeable that the sheriff did not insist that they hand over their guns. With little else to do, Cobb watched for a while and then moved on.

A short time later he wandered down the street again to find a group of people gathered around a man lying on the boardwalk outside the sheriff's office. Out of nothing else than idle curiosity, he crossed the street and joined them.

The man lying on the boardwalk was apparently one of the prison guards and he gathered that the man bending over and examining him was the doctor. Eventually the doctor slowly stood up and shook his head as he spoke to the sheriff.

'Dead!' he pronounced. 'Heart attack I'd say.'

'Hell!' oathed the sheriff. 'I guess I'll have to wire Denver and tell 'em. It'll mean that the men I've got can't be taken away an' that means waitin' until they send someone else. Why'd he have to go an' die on me?'

'I don't suppose he intended to die on you,' said Cobb. 'People don't usually go around dying on others intentionally. I'm surprised they sent old men like him and the other one.'

'Yeh, maybe he didn't,' muttered the sheriff. 'It's just bloody inconvenient, that's all. He could've waited until they'd left. I'll have to get the undertaker to move the body. I sure can't leave him lyin' here.'

'I suppose there's some ordinance about littering the streets,' said Cobb, sarcastically.

'Very funny, Cobb,' grunted the sheriff. 'If you've

come for your guns you'll have to wait until the mornin'.' He looked at one of the other men gathered round. 'Sam, you go and get John Scarman to come and collect him. Tell him not to do anythin' yet. I'll have to find out what Denver want doin' with the body. I'm goin' over to the telegraph office.'

At about eight o'clock that evening Cobb was propping up the counter of Kate's Bar, wondering if he could again afford three dollars for a few minutes with Maureen. He was joined by the surviving prison guard who looked very dejected.

'Sorry to hear about your partner,' said Cobb. 'I guess these things happen though.'

'I suppose so,' muttered the guard. 'It's a pity though, me and Tom had been together a long time. More like brothers we were.' He took a long drink of his beer and looked around. 'Have you seen the sheriff?'

'Not since he went off to send a wire to Denver,' said Cobb. 'What will you do now?'

'Wait here until they send a replacement I suppose,' grunted the guard. 'I can't take five men on my own, that's for sure.'

'Do you do this kind of thing regularly?' asked Cobb.

'All the time,' replied the guard. 'Me an' Tom have been doin' it for more than twenty years and we've never lost a client yet. At least he wasn't married and had no family as far as I know.'

At that moment the sheriff walked in, obviously looking for someone. That someone appeared to be the prison guard.

'Bad news,' he grunted, slouching across the counter and grasping the glass of beer which suddenly appeared in front of him. 'Denver says you have to take them on your own.'

'On my own!' exclaimed the guard. 'I can't manage five of them on my own.'

'Well, since I can't spare nobody to go with you, they say you have to,' said the sheriff. 'The only other thing they suggested was a volunteer to ride with you. I've already asked around an' there ain't no volunteers and there's certainly not that many folk as I'd trust with the job. Oh, an' they say Tom is to be buried here.'

'I guessed they'd say that,' said the guard. 'Bloody typical. Leave a man where he falls just so long as it don't mean no trouble for them in Denver. Good job he didn't have any family.'

'You never asked me to volunteer for the job,' said Cobb. 'Were they offering payment?'

'I thought about you but I didn't think you'd be interested,' said the sheriff.

'Or was it because your Mr Watson wouldn't approve?' sneered Cobb.

'This kind of thing ain't got nothin' to do with him,' the sheriff muttered. 'Anyhow, Denver's north-west of here an' you are headed east.'

'I'm headed which ever way takes my fancy,' said Cobb. 'If you're paying enough to ride shotgun with the prisoners, it just might be that I could fancy heading north-west.'

The sheriff looked at Cobb for a while and then slowly nodded. 'Yeh, it could be that you're just the man for the job. Yeh, I'd say you bein' an ex-army major made you the ideal person. How about fifty dollars?'

'How about if I just keep on riding east?' said Cobb.

'Well fifty dollars is what they suggested an' it sure ain't bad money for about one week's work,' said the sheriff. 'It wasn't my idea. Denver suggest that much.'

'And how long should it take to reach the prison?' Cobb asked the guard.

'Like the sheriff said, the best part of a week,' replied the guard. 'That's provided we don't hit any problems.'

'Such as someone trying to free them?'

'No, I wasn't thinking of that,' said the guard. 'I mean the wagon getting stuck, the state of any rivers we have to cross, land slides, that type of thing.'

'And what would you do if somebody did try to set them free?' asked Cobb.

'Mister!' sighed the guard. 'Denver might be offering fifty dollars to a volunteer but they sure don't pay the likes of me, who do this kind of thing for a living, that kind of money. Tom and me always said that if something like that was to happen we sure wouldn't fight. As far as I'm concerned anyone who so much as says *boo* to me can have any prisoners I've got.' He laughed drily. 'Strange thing is it's never happened yet, even though there have been a few very well-known prisoners in my care.'

'Sheriff,' said Cobb, 'if you can talk Denver into making it one hundred dollars, you have your volunteer.'

'As far as I'm concerned it'll be money well spent,' said the sheriff. 'OK I'll send another wire, but it is a bit late. I might not get an answer until the mornin'.'

'I'm in no hurry,' replied Cobb. 'I'm sure an extra fifty dollars is not going to stretch the finances of the state too far.'

The sheriff muttered something which Cobb did not catch, drained his glass and left. The guard remained silent for a while and then looked at Cobb.

'So you were a major in the army?' he said. 'I was in the army too before I took up this job. To be honest I don't have that much time for officers. I was a sergeant.'

'Almost every sergeant I ever met didn't think much of their officers,' said Cobb. 'They seemed to think that we didn't know what we were talking about. Still, that doesn't matter, neither of us is in the army now, so I suppose that makes us equal. If I do get this job, I can assure you I won't try to pull rank. As far as I'm concerned you'll be in command.'

'Yeh?' said the guard, giving Cobb a hostile stare. 'I hope you remember that. OK, Major, since it'll only be for about a week, I guess I can live with it.' He too drained his glass and turned to leave. 'I reckon Denver will agree to your price,' he continued. 'I wonder if they'd pay me that much if I refused to take those men?'

The guard left and almost immediately another man joined Cobb. Cobb recognized him as Lance Watson's foreman. For a while the foreman studiously avoided any eye contact with Cobb but eventually he turned and stared at him.

'Mr Watson didn't like the way you talked to him,' he said. 'He sent me into town to make sure you got the message about leavin'.'

'I got the message,' replied Cobb. 'I was leaving anyway.'

'I hear the sheriff asked you about ridin' shotgun on the prison wagon,' said the foreman. 'I don't think that would be a very wise thing to do.'

'Oh, and why is that?' asked Cobb. 'Is it because he resents me being offered any kind of work? News travels fast. It's only just been suggested that I take the job.'

'There's nothin' happens in Wentworth that Mr Watson doesn't get to hear about,' said the foreman. 'Sometimes he gets to hear about things even before they've happened.'

'So the telegraph clerk is in his pay,' said Cobb with a shrug. 'There's nothing new in that.'

'I wouldn't know about things like that,' said the foreman. 'All I'm tellin' you is that it wouldn't be wise to take the job.'

'Mister,' said Cobb with a heavy sigh. 'I hadn't actually decided on taking the job. However, I do not like being threatened, for whatever reason. You can run back to your master and inform him that I am riding with the prison wagon.'

The foreman looked Cobb up and down for a few moments and then sneered. 'I guess it's your funeral. Just don't say you wasn't warned.'

'I won't,' assured Cobb. 'Now, if you don't mind, I have an appointment with a very pretty bar girl.'

'Make the most of it,' said the foreman with a derisory laugh. He took his glass and wandered across the room where he joined three other men at a table. It was obvious that the main topic of conversation was Cobb as all four men looked at him and laughed amongst themselves and then at him.

Cobb found Maureen and spent a very pleasant half hour with her, during which time he asked her about Lance Watson and his foreman.

'All I know is that Lance Watson is not a man to be crossed,' she said. 'I wouldn't trust that foreman of his not to steal a candy from a baby either.' She thought for a moment. 'Come to think of it that man Smith was also interested in Lance Watson. I don't know why, he never really said and I never ask questions. It isn't healthy to ask too many questions, especially where they concern Mr Watson.'

'Smith again,' said Cobb. 'It's strange how he keeps cropping up. It's also very strange that he should disappear so quickly. I wonder if there is a connection between them?'

'Don't ask me and I don't want to know,' replied Maureen. Cobb returned to the bar to find the sheriff looking for him.

'OK, you got yourself a job,' said the sheriff. 'I was surprised they agreed so readily. You get your money when the prisoners are delivered.'

'I would have preferred the cash up front,' said Cobb.

'They ain't that stupid,' said the sheriff with a dry laugh. 'If you get the money first there's nothin' to stop you just ridin' out, is there?'

'I suppose not,' agreed Cobb. 'OK, I'll take the job. There is just one thing I'm very curious about. Watson's foreman was in here some time ago . . .' He looked about but could not see the foreman. 'It seems that Watson had heard about me being offered the job even before you asked me. To me that says that you had already decided before I volunteered. . . .' The sheriff simply shrugged but said nothing 'That isn't what bothers me, though, nor how Watson found out. It was that foreman of his warning me off the job. Now why should he do something like that?'

'Search me,' said the sheriff.

'Is there any connection between the men you have in jail and Watson?'

'None that I know of,' replied the sheriff.

'None that you know of,' said Cobb. 'Or at least none that you are prepared to admit to. I talked to Maureen again and it appears that the mysterious Mr Smith also asked about Watson and those men. I can't help but wonder.'

'Cobb,' sighed the sheriff. 'If you're lookin' for an excuse to get out of doin' this, don't bother. You either want the job or you don't.'

'Don't get all het-up,' said Cobb. 'I've already said I'll do it. I'd just like to know why that foreman tried to warn me off, that's all. It was almost as if he knew that something was going to happen.'

'Well there's no reason as far as I'm concerned,' said the sheriff. 'I'll sure try to find out just what Watson is up to, though.'

Cobb shook his head and sighed. 'Don't bother. He wouldn't tell you unless he wanted you to know. What time do you want me in the morning?'

'First light,' said the sheriff. 'I'll have your guns ready an' waitin'.'

Cobb returned to Rose Golightly's rooming-house to discover that he had the place to himself. The four men who had been there had apparently moved out to Lance Watson's ranch. In a way he was grateful to have the place to himself.

Cobb reckoned that it was shortly after midnight when he became aware of someone moving about outside. Strangely, he found that he was not too surprised. He had had the feeling that perhaps Lance Watson wanted to drive home the point of him leaving. He slipped out of his bed, rearranged it to make it look like he was still sleeping and then waited, secreting himself behind a large locker in a corner.

A few minutes later the door slowly opened and two shadowy figures slipped silently into the room. For a few moments they stood at the foot of his bunk until eventually one of them stepped forward. The brief glint of a knife-blade told Cobb exactly what was about to happen. The man raised his arm and brought the knife down into the bundle in the bed. This was repeated twice more before either man realized things were not quite as they appeared.

'I'm over here!' hissed Cobb. 'Sorry to disappoint you.'

'Bastard!' snarled one of the men, a voice Cobb thought he recognized as belonging to the foreman.

'Try doing that against a man who is also armed with a knife,' Cobb hissed again. He did have a knife but it was only a small one he used for cutting meat and vegetables. He had serious doubts as to whether it would be that effective in a fight.

'Let's get out of here!' rasped the second man. 'He don't pay enough for me to murder anyone.' Both men suddenly turned and clattered out of the door. Cobb made no attempt to follow, he knew very well that nobody would believe him. His only surprise was that neither man had tried to shoot him.

'I suppose that's one advantage of having an ordinance against the carrying of guns,' he said to himself.

Reasonably confident that there would be no other attempt on his life again that night, Cobb returned to his bunk and it was not long before he was asleep.

THREE

It seemed to Cobb that almost the entire population of Wentworth had turned out to witness the departure of the outlaws, most standing a respectful distance away, as if expecting the men to try and make a break for it. In actual fact the outlaws were strangely silent, although they did glare at Cobb with obvious hatred when he went inside the jail. He did not mind that, he was used to it.

'You almost had a murder on your hands last night,' said Cobb to the sheriff as he was handed his guns. 'Watson's foreman and another man came into the rooming-house just after midnight and tried to kill me with a knife.'

'Can you prove that?' grunted the sheriff, obviously not at all interested. 'Attempted murder is a very serious accusation.'

'Unfortunately I can't,' admitted Cobb. 'I know who it was though and I have the feeling that you also know.'

'I don't know nothin',' snarled the sheriff. 'Anyhow, I have a vested interest in keepin' you alive, at least until you're out of my territory. If they had killed you that would have meant that my prisoners would have to stay here.'

'I have the feeling that making sure those prisoners don't leave is exactly what they want,' said Cobb. 'I don't suppose there's any possibility that that guard was murdered and didn't die of a heart attack?'

'None at all,' said the sheriff. 'I was with him when it happened. He complained of feeling ill and then suddenly collapsed. Anyhow, Doc Murdoch knows what he's doing. He's seen folk die of heart attacks before so he ought to know.'

'It was very convenient though,' said Cobb. 'If I'm right and somebody like Watson, for reasons we don't yet know, wanted to make sure that those men were not transported to prison, that heart attack came just at the right time. Perhaps I am just being suspicious, but I don't believe in coincidences like that.'

'Well you'd better believe in 'em this time 'cos that's the way it happened,' muttered the sheriff. 'And I wouldn't go around making accusations like that about Lance Watson if I was you. Like I said before, Lance Watson packs a lot of clout in this part of the world and in Denver.'

'That doesn't make him an honest man though,' said Cobb. 'I had a general once who turned out to be as crooked as any outlaw. It turned out he was selling guns to the Indians.'

'As far as I'm concerned, all soldiers are crooked,' muttered the sheriff. 'When they was stationed here they was more trouble than any outlaws. The officers weren't much better either.'

'That's just your opinion,' said Cobb. 'Now, since I am to transport these outlaws to prison, it'd be handy to know just what they've done.'

'Oh, just the usual,' replied the sheriff in a very matter-of-fact way. 'Murder, rape, robbery, you know the kind of thing.'

'They sound like pleasant characters,' said Cobb. 'I still think there's a connection between them and Watson though.'

'There's none that I know of,' said the sheriff. 'Even if there was, I'd forget it if I was you. The last job they did was to rob a bank at Pine Falls. They were supposed to have got away with over ten thousand dollars, but it has never been recovered. That was sort of strange, I have to admit. That robbery took place just ten days before they came here but they certainly didn't have that kind of money on them. In fact they only had twelve dollars between 'em. They reckon there was six of 'em in that robbery, but only five of 'em turned up here.'

'Could that be the connection?' asked Cobb. 'The money from the robbery, I mean. Of course, there was a sixth man here, the one Maureen saw in Kate's Bar who called himself Smith.'

'How the hell should I know if there's a connection or not?' snorted the sheriff. 'I don't even care if there is just as long as they're taken well away from Wentworth. It also seems that the only person in Wentworth to see this Smith was her. I wouldn't put too much store by her story. OK, let's get them out of my jail. The sooner they're gone the better as far as I'm concerned.'

The five outlaws, shackled together by their ankles

and with individual chains to their wrists, were led from the jail and bundled into the prison wagon where the guard, whose name was Silas, fixed their leg-chains to stout rings in the floor. When he had finished he slammed the heavy door, locked it firmly and went round the cage testing the bars.

'Ain't no man ever escaped from that,' he announced to Cobb, with some pride. 'Now remember what you said, Major,' he continued. 'You take your orders from me.'

'The name's Cobb,' said Cobb. 'I'm not a major any longer and yes, you're in charge.'

'Just remember that,' muttered Silas. 'As far as I'm concerned I'll call you Major. Once an army officer, always an army officer I say.'

'Suit yourself, *Sergeant*,' replied Cobb. Silas muttered something which Cobb did not quite catch but gathered was not very complimentary. 'Now, do you want me to ride up with you or tag along on my horse?'

'I don't care,' replied Silas. 'I can live quite happily with my own company. OK, let's go!' He climbed aboard the wagon and urged the two horses drawing it, forward. 'Nice meetin' you,' he said to the sheriff. 'I hope you don't take offence when I say I hope we never meet again.'

'None taken,' assured the sheriff. 'The feelin's mutual. Nothin' personal.'

They rode in almost total silence for about half an hour before Cobb pulled alongside Silas. 'What happened to your partner, Tom?' he asked.

'What's it to you, *Major*?' grunted Silas. 'They buried him last night an' I didn't see you there. As a matter of fact there was nobody there 'ceptin' me, the sheriff, the undertaker an' the preacher. Not that I expected anybody else.'

'What will you do now?' asked Cobb. 'Get a new partner?'

'Maybe, maybe not,' said Silas. 'Me an' Tom had been talkin' about packin' this in anyhow. It's just a pity he had to go like that before we did. No, I reckon this is goin' to be my last trip. I've got my eye on a small farm belongin' to a widder-woman near Denver.'

'Does that include the widow?' asked Cobb, with a broad grin.

'Well, I'll put it this way,' said Silas. 'She's made it pretty damned plain that if I want the farm she has to go along with it.'

'It sounds like a good deal,' said Cobb. 'Perhaps I should find myself a woman like that.'

He dropped back slightly and looked into the cage. The response from two of the outlaws was to spit at him. Other than that they remained silent.

Cobb dropped back even further and rode behind the wagon from where he surveyed the surrounding hills. He was troubled. For some time he had had the feeling that they were being followed, but there was no sign of anyone. He eventually tried putting it down to his imagination, but without much success.

There were two brief stops during the day. The first was at about midday alongside a river where the prisoners were let out of the wagon – still manacled together – and allowed to attend to the calls of nature and to drink from the river. The second stop was at a small waterhole at mid-afternoon simply to allow the horses to drink. On both occasions, still troubled by the feeling that they were being followed, Cobb took the opportunity to climb to the top of some high ground and survey the direction from which they had come. On neither occasion did he see anyone.

'Yeh, I get that feelin' too sometimes,' said Silas when Cobb told him of his feelings as they eventually stopped alongside a small stream for the night. 'Usually it depends on how valuable my cargo is. Somebody who is famous is always likely to have friends who want to help for some reason. Most don't fall into that category an' nobody don't care what the hell happens to 'em. When you've been doin' this kind of thing for a long time you learn how to ignore it. It ain't often there is anybody there. In fact I can only remember three times when there was. Twice it turned out to be Indians just bein' curious, but they left us alone, an' the other time it was some drifter who just happened to be goin' the same way.'

'You are probably right,' said Cobb. He spoke to one of the prisoners as they were allowed out of the wagon. 'Do you know a man named Smith?'

'I know hundreds of Smiths,' replied the outlaw. 'An' hundreds of Joneses too. What's so particular about this Smith?'

'I don't know, I've never met him,' said Cobb. 'All I know is there was a man named Smith who seemed to be very interested in you back in Wentworth. There were supposed to be six of you who were in that robbery in Pine Falls. I wondered if it might be him.'

The man smiled and shook his head. 'Naw, his name warn't Smith.'

'Major, you can collect some wood an' brush for a fire,' said Silas. 'I'll get some food goin'. I ain't much of a cook but it's all any of you is goin' to get.' He lifted the seat at the front of the wagon and took out two bags. The one contained dried beans and the other some dried, unidentifiable, meat. He emptied both into a large pot, added some water and, when Cobb had collected the wood and lit the fire, placed it over. 'This'll take a couple of hours,' he continued. 'If you want anythin' more fancy or fresh, Major, you'll have get out there an' kill it yourself. There's deer up there somewhere, I heard one callin' just now.'

'I'll eat what everyone else eats,' said Cobb. 'I dare say I've eaten far worse in the army.'

'If you'd been an ordinary soldier I might agree,' sneered Silas. 'I never yet met an officer what didn't eat better'n his men though. I even had me a captain once who always carried bottles of wine just for his own use. There we'd be, in the middle of a desert with nothin' but what was in our canteens an' there he'd be with his bottle of wine. He never even offered any to his lieutenant.'

'He probably knew he wouldn't appreciate good wine,' said Cobb. 'I don't happen to have any wine or even whiskey with me at the moment, so I suppose I'll have to make do with whatever you drink.'

'Water!' grunted Silas. 'Water straight from the river.'

With nothing better to do whilst waiting for the meal and after making certain that the prisoners could not escape, Cobb rode to the top of a nearby hill, still unable to shake the feeling of being followed.

From the hill, Cobb had a good view all around and at first there was no obvious signs of life. However, after a short time he became quite convinced that there was someone – or at least something – amongst a group of rocks about two hundred yards away. His initial impulse was to ride down and take a look, but he resisted. As he looked about he began to realize that his imagination was working overtime. Suddenly, everywhere he looked there appeared to be movement.

Pull yourself together! he said to himself. You're beginning to see things. You'll soon convince yourself that there's someone behind every rock. He returned to the wagon where Silas grinned at him.

'Don't tell me,' said Silas without being told. 'You've just seen hundreds of folk out there, all hidin'.' Cobb nodded, feeling rather foolish. 'That's how it gets you sometimes,' continued Silas. 'Best thing to do is just ignore it. There sure ain't much you can do about it if there is.'

'Don't you have the feeling we're being followed?' asked Cobb.

'Can't say as I do,' said Silas. 'I did when I first started on this business but not now. Anyhow, if there is an' they're out to free this lot they wouldn't try nothin' until sundown when they can pinpoint us by the light of the fire. That way they can see us but we can't see them.'

'And doesn't the thought bother you?'

'No,' shrugged Silas. 'If there is anybody out there

I don't reckon they would kill me. They probably know I wouldn't put up no fight. Like I said before, if somebody wants 'em that bad they can have 'em. They don't pay me enough to make it worthwhile riskin' my life. Anyhow, standard instructions are not to risk gettin' killed.'

'But I've got a hundred dollars at the end of this and I don't want to lose it,' said Cobb.

'Then you put up a fight if you want, but just leave me out of it,' said Silas.

Cobb nodded. Silas's attitude and apparent instructions did make sense. No outlaw was worth risking one's life for. However, despite having been on the verge of seeing gunmen everywhere, he was still quite certain that there was someone out there. Despite being convinced that they were being followed, he did not think there was more than one. Had there been, he was quite sure that they would have made some move by that time.

'What about the other man who was with you?' he said to one of the prisoners. 'I suppose he has the money from the bank.'

'If he had, he sure wouldn't be the one you seem to think might be followin' us,' replied the man. 'I know damned well that if it had been me I'd've been well away from here by now.'

'And leave your friends to rot in prison?' said Cobb.

'Too damned right,' said one of the others. 'Any one of us would take the money and run like hell.'

'So much for friendship and honour,' said Cobb. 'OK, I'll go along with what you say. That doesn't alter the fact that I am quite sure there's somebody out there and since he can't be interested in me or Silas here, as neither of us has much money on us, his interest must be in you. Now, I ask myself just why should anyone be that interested? I agree that if he was the sixth man and had the money he would probably not bother. That tells me that he does not have the money and does not know where it is. That again tells me that if he doesn't know, then either one or all of you do. Ten thousand dollars is a lot of money and I know men who would go almost to the ends of the earth to get it. I would also like to know why someone back in Wentworth should try to kill me other than knowing it would mean that you would have stayed there?'

'I hear you was a major in the army,' said the first outlaw. 'That makes you a man what's had book-learnin', which makes you too clever for the likes of us. You just carry on thinkin', Major, a bullet don't know the difference.'

'So you do know who is out there?' said Cobb.

'I didn't say that,' said the outlaw. 'Sure, if there is somebody then I guess we all got a pretty good idea just who it is.'

'Smith?' asked Cobb. There was a noticeable change in the expression of the outlaw and he shook his head. 'So you do know the Smith I'm talking about,' continued Cobb. 'Out of all the hundreds of Smiths you say you know, you know exactly who I mean. I don't think he's the man who was with you in Pine Falls either. That means that there could be two of them out there. They could team up.'

'Major,' said the man. 'We don't have no idea who this feller Smith is. All we know is that he's been

followin' us for some time now. We don't even know
what he looks like. All he's done is follow us but don't
do nothin'. He makes us more nervous than he does
you.'

'Then how do you know about him?'

'It's always the same,' replied the man. 'We ride
into a town an' before long there's someone tellin' us
that there'a a man called Smith lookin' for us. That's
all he seems to do, make sure we know he's around
an' then leave. We ain't never seen or heard him an'
so far he ain't tried to do nothin', but he's always
there. We've even tried lookin' for him but we ain't
never found him. It's almost as if he's a ghost.'

'And why should any man follow you like that?'
asked Cobb. 'You must have some idea.'

'We can't think of no reason,' said the man.

'You have apparently committed murder,' said
Cobb. 'Perhaps he's out to get revenge.'

'Then he sure is takin' his time about it,' shrugged
the man. 'He's had more'n enough chances.'

Cobb gave up on the idea of questioning the men
any further. It was quite obvious that they either did
not know Smith or were, for some reason, refusing to
say. He had the feeling that their claim of not knowing Smith had a ring of truth about it, which simply
served to make him all the more curious.

Silas, who had been listening, reached into the
box under the seat of the wagon and handed Cobb
five pieces of paper. They were the official documents he had been given to transport the outlaws.
Each one contained details of each man, together
with a list of known crimes and associates. The list of
known associates was very limited and was mainly

confined to each other. Cobb settled himself to read the documents whilst they waited for their meal to cook.

'Clayton Branagan,' he read out loud. 'Two murders, at least one rape and two robberies which can be proved. Reward two thousand dollars. Which one of you is Branagan?'

'Me,' replied the outlaw who had so far been the most talkative. 'I'm surprised they're only offerin' two thousand. I reckon I'm worth double that.'

'Sam Strong,' continued Cobb. 'One murder, no known rapes, three bank robberies, two robberies of stores and arson. Fifteen hundred dollars.'

'Present and correct, *sir!*' sneered one of the others. 'You can add to that two years in military prison followed by dishonourable discharge from the army for stealin' guns. That's somethin' you know a lot about, ain't it, *Major?* Dishonourable discharge. I hear tell you was cashiered as well. I always thought that was strange. Ordinary soldiers are given a dishonourable discharge, officers are always *cashiered.* I don't know what the difference is, but I guess bein' cashiered sounds better.'

Cobb ignored the man and continued. 'Clenton Brakespeare. That's a high-class sounding name, Brakespeare.'

'I didn't choose it,' muttered the owner of that name. 'I guess if you call the slums along the docks of the East River in New York high class, then I am.'

'You're a long way from home,' observed Cobb. 'Just like me; I'm from Boston. I see you did three years in prison for robbery, now wanted for one suspected murder, four bank robberies and arson.

Fifteen hundred. Michael Foley, known as Three Fingers Foley because you have only three fingers on your left hand. What happened to the other two, did somebody find them where they shouldn't have been?' Three Fingers held up his hand and grunted. 'One bank robbery, two rapes and general mayhem. You're only worth seven hundred fifty dollars.'

'I'm not as ambitious as the others,' said Foley.

'Now here's a really fancy-sounding name,' continued Cobb. 'James Arbuthnot Trevelian, known as Cornwall Jimmy. Cornwall, that's in England isn't it?'

'That's what my ma an' pa reckoned,' said Trevelian. 'That's where they came from. I was born an' raised in Kansas. I was always known as Cornwall Jimmy even when I was a kid.'

'You seem to be a beginner at this game,' continued Cobb. 'Although you were apparently involved in a train robbery. Apart from that, your specialty seems to be blowing things up and lighting fires. Five hundred dollars.'

'OK *Major*,' sneered Branagan. 'So now you know all about us, for all the good it'll do you.'

'I know what these pieces of paper say about you,' said Cobb. 'I don't really know all about you and I can't say that I'm that interested. I'm more interested in just why somebody should try to kill me in Wentworth. There's no reason at all as far as I can see, I know I didn't upset anyone there. I think someone wanted to make sure you were not transported to prison.'

'And why should they want to do that?' asked Sam Strong.

'I can think of ten thousand reasons,' said Cobb.

'The money from that bank,' said Strong. 'That's what they reckon we took. I don't reckon it was that much. I know none of us ain't much with countin' an' book-learnin' but I reckon it was nearer six thousand. I reckon the owner of that bank used the robbery as an excuse to get his hands on some of his own money. I had it happen to me once before. He'd been takin' money an' used the robbery to cover it up. He didn't make a very good job of it though, 'cos they found out.'

'Six thousand or ten thousand, it's still a lot of money,' said Cobb. 'What did you do with it?'

'Spent it!' sneered Strong. 'What else is money for?'

'That's a lot of money to spend in ten days,' said Cobb. 'I think you hid it somewhere. Somewhere the man who was with you doesn't know about and I think he could be the one who is following right now.'

'I thought you said it was this Smith,' said Branagan.

'Perhaps they are one and the same,' said Cobb. 'I'm confusing myself, I don't really know what I think. Whichever of them it is, I do think we'll find out for sure pretty soon now. It could be that he'll kill you. You are all sitting targets.'

'And you,' said Branagan.

'But I don't know where the money is,' said Cobb. 'And I won't be the one locked in a cage.'

'His bullet won't know that,' said Branagan.

FOUR

As darkness closed in, Cobb started to feel increasingly uneasy and several times checked that his guns were loaded, much to the amusement of Silas. Silas himself appeared totally unconcerned, stressing that it was probably all imagination on Cobb's part. Cobb was quite convinced that it was anything but his imagination.

However, it was quite plain that Silas was used to taking no chances regarding the possible escape of his prisoners. To this end he ordered them to sit around a tree and then he produced a stout padlock and joined the two ends of the chain. This meant that their only means of escape lay in chopping down the tree. Cobb had to admit that it was a simple but very effective method and that he would not have thought of such a thing. Simple it might have been, but it did nothing to quell Cobb's feeling of unease.

The result was that Cobb spent a sleepless night, his imagination working overtime. The slightest sound had him grabbing his rifle, convinced that someone was close by. On each occasion it appeared that it had in fact been nothing more than his imag-

ination or possibly some nocturnal animal. After a
very long night, he had never been more thankful to
see dawn break.

'Told you you was imaginin' things, Major,' said
Silas. 'I don't reckon you got much sleep last night.'

'If somebody is going to try to kill me,' said Cobb,
'I'd like to be awake when it happens. I have to admit
that I am very surprised that nothing did happen
though. No matter what you say I still think there's
somebody out there. They might even be watching us
right now.'

'Maybe so,' said Silas. 'If all they do is watch, then
we've got nothin' to worry about. It sure looks like
you lost sleep for nothin' though,' He unlocked the
chain and allowed the prisoners to drink from the
stream and attend the call of nature. 'That's all you
get until tonight,' he told them. 'One meal a day is
all the State says you're allowed. You're lucky to get
that. There was a time when they didn't provide prisoners with any food.'

'You call that shit you gave us food?' muttered
Clayton Branagan.

'It's a darn sight better'n you'll get in prison,' said
Silas. 'I wouldn't feed a pig on what you'll get in
there. OK, into the wagon, we've still got a few days
to go.'

Cobb had to admit to himself that he felt rather
foolish about his insistence that they were being
followed. If there had been someone, the previous
night would have been an ideal opportunity to
attack. However, the feeling persisted and he was all
the more curious as to why nothing had happened.
He helped Silas secure the men in the wagon and

then mounted his horse. In a final gesture of what amounted to little more than self-assurance, he rode to the top of a nearby ridge. . . .

Cobb did not actually hear anything, but he certainly felt a searing pain in his head and he vaguely remembered hitting the ground. Although very painful, the shot did not make him lose consciousness but before he could react fully there was a figure standing over him with a gun aimed at his head. He recognized the sneering features of Lance Watson's foreman.

'This is the end of the line for you, *Major*!' sneered the foreman. He took slow and careful aim, obviously intent on making certain that Cobb would be killed this time.

Cobb certainly heard the next shot and to say that he was surprised when a bullet did not thud into his head would be something of an understatement. For a brief moment the foreman stared unseeingly at his intended victim before he suddenly collapsed on the ground. Cobb was even more surprised when, on glancing at Silas, he saw that the guard was not the one responsible for the shot. He looked up at a rock just in time to see a figure disappearing.

He raised himself to his elbow and looked at the body of the foreman. There was no doubting that he was dead. Blood oozed from a hole in the side of his head. By that time Silas was at his side and Cobb felt very sick and giddy.

'I told you there was somebody there, Sergeant!' he managed to say.

'Yeh, you was right, I was wrong, Major!' replied

Silas. 'I guess that's why they made you an officer, you know these things.'

When Cobb again came to, he discovered that he was strapped on to the wooden seat of the wagon. Silas looked at him and grinned.

'I guess that made up for the sleep you didn't get last night,' he said.

'How long have I been out?' asked Cobb.

'Oh, at least five hours, maybe even more,' said Silas. 'I cleaned up your head as best I could. You'll live, it's nothin' more'n a deep scratch, I've seen worse.'

Cobb twisted round and, with a certain amount of relief, saw that the prisoners were still in the wagon. He also noted that there was a body across his horse, which was tethered behind the wagon: the body of Watson's foreman.

'I have the feeling that we have just discovered who the sixth man in the bank robbery was,' said Cobb. 'I also think I know who the man was who saved my life, but I don't know why.'

'This feller you call Smith,' said Silas. 'Sure, that makes sense I suppose.'

'I'm glad it makes sense to someone,' grunted Cobb. 'It certainly does not make much sense to me.' He spoke to the men in the wagon. 'I'd say your Mr Smith was just letting you know that he is still around.'

'We know,' replied Branagan. 'We also know that he's followin' us right now. We've all seen him three or four times, not more'n a hundred yards behind.'

Cobb looked back but could not see any sign of the mysterious Mr Smith.

'I assume that Lance Watson's foreman, the man who attacked me, was also the sixth man at that robbery. What was his name? I never did find out.'

'He ain't got much use for a name now,' said Branagan. 'You can assume what the hell you like, Major. It won't make any difference to him now, will it?'

'I suppose not,' admitted Cobb. 'I just wish somebody would tell me what the hell is going on. I am almost certain that this other man is the one who calls himself Smith, the same one who always lets you know that he's around. He's plainly no friend of yours but on the other hand he doesn't seem to want to kill you. Are you sure you don't know who he really is or what he wants from you? I'd like to thank him for saving my life.'

'I guess everybody is entitled to one mistake,' said Sam Strong, with a broad grin. 'He just made his by not killin' you while he had the chance.'

'A mistake as far as you're concerned, you mean,' said Cobb. 'If it hadn't been for him you might have been free men now. Still, I don't think we'll be bothered by anyone trying to free you now and I think you are all more scared of Mr Smith than you are prepared to admit.'

'I'll admit it, Major,' said James Arbuthnott Trevelian – Cornwall Jimmy. 'He scares the shit out of me. I just wish he'd *do* somethin'.'

'Yeh, me, too,' admitted Three Fingers Foley. 'What the hell *does* he want? As far as I know I've never seen him in my life. This is the first time he's actually showed himself an' he sure ain't nobody I recognize.'

'None of us ain't never seen him before,' said Branagan. 'Maybe you should find out who the hell he is and what he wants, Major. At least you now know where he is.'

'I might just do that,' said Cobb as he turned to face the way they were going. 'He seems to know exactly what he's doing though, so I suspect getting anywhere near him will not be easy.'

'There's a small tradin' post not far ahead,' said Silas. 'We'll pull up there for an hour. I know the man who runs it, name of Luke Mostyn. His woman can have a look at that head of yours while we're there. She also rents herself out to weary travellers – with her old man's blessin' of course.' He turned and laughed at the men in the wagon. 'Not that you lot will be able to take her up on it. She charges one dollar a time an' strictly cash. You ain't got one dollar between you an' I sure as hell ain't payin' for you. You've got time if the fancy takes you, Major.'

'I can imagine what she's like as well,' said Cobb. 'I think I'll give such pleasures a miss for once. Abstinence is supposed to be good for the soul, they tell me. At least that's what my mother used to say.'

'Mine too,' said Silas with a coarse laugh 'Accordin' to my pa, the number of times she made him abstain he must have had one hell of a good soul. I guess that was why he suddenly upped an' left us one day. They say he took Widder Brown with him an' even us kids knew that she didn't have no soul at all. She even used to try an' get us boys to go with her. I guess we was too young to really appreciate it all though, at least I was. I thought it was real dirty, but I learned.'

An hour later and still, apparently, with Mr Smith continuing to follow, they reached the trading post. The first thing that struck Cobb was that the woman was nothing like he had expected. He had assumed that she would be much like most other women living in isolated homesteads, fat, dirty and ugly. She was, in fact, young, slim and quite good looking, although she certainly gave the impression that soap and water were infrequent visitors to her skin. Despite her obvious attraction, he refused the blatant offer to sample the delights of her body.

She did not appear upset by his refusal and expertly cleaned up his wound and bandaged it. Luke Mostyn, her husband, appeared considerably older than her claimed twenty-two years, which made him about the same age as Cobb. Luke Mostyn too appeared to have an aversion to soap and water.

There was an offer to supply them all with food, but when both Cobb and Silas stirred the pot hanging over an open fire and discovered that the meat content of the stew was little more than gristle and the smell was reminiscent of long-decaying flesh, both refused.

Cobb had the feeling that the meat in the stew was the scrapings off the animal hides and furs which lay in piles around the building, attracting thousands of flies and giving the whole place the foul stench of a derelict mule-skinner's yard he had once encountered. Several times Cobb ventured outside, mainly to escape the smell which made him feel sick, but partly to see if there was any sign of Smith, which there was not and he was not too surprised.

He realized that the comment made by Branagan,

that he now knew where Smith was and ought to find out just what he wanted, had been nothing more than a throw-away remark, but it had sown the seed of an idea which slowly developed in his mind. Eventually Silas declared that it was time to leave and urged the horses drawing the wagon forward.

About ten minutes after the wagon had left the trading post a lone rider slowly approached and dismounted. The man was quite small and very wiry and obviously not in too much of hurry as he stopped briefly to allow his horse to drink. It was as the man himself immersed his head into the trough of water that he suddenly became aware of somebody standing over him.

'I wouldn't go for that gun of yours,' rasped the figure. 'Just stand up and turn around, Mr Smith.' Smith did not move. In fact he kept his face immersed in the water for some considerable time, holding his breath. Quite suddenly, he did move.

Cobb, being slightly to one side of Smith, had not noticed the hand furthest away from him slowly grasping a ladle.

In almost one movement Smith suddenly stood up straight, the ladle scooped some water and this was thrown, very accurately, into Cobb's face. Although blinded only for a second, it was long enough for Smith's bony knee to jerk into Cobb's groin. The result was very painful causing Cobb to double up. His gun was ripped from his hand and once again the bony knee jerked upwards, this time smashing into Cobb's face. When Cobb recovered, Smith was on his horse and racing back in the direction he had come. Cobb cursed loudly and recovered his gun which was lying a few yards away. He was conscious of blood streaming from his nose.

'Better let me look at that,' said Mrs Mostyn. 'It seems to me you've got some learnin' to do.'

'Learning?' queried Cobb, trying to staunch the blood by wiping his sleeve across his face.

'Yeh, about dirty fightin',' she laughed. 'Silas reckoned you was an officer in the army which also makes you a gentleman I suppose. At least you're more of a gentleman than most folk in these parts. The trouble with gentlemen is that they don't know how to fight dirty, they expect other folk to "play by the rules" as they say. The trouble is most folk out this way don't know what the rules are supposed to be so how can they be expected to keep to 'em? Come on inside, let's get you cleaned up again.'

'I'll sit out here,' said Cobb, not wanting to go inside to the smell. The woman shrugged and filled the ladle with water. She found a rather soiled rag, soaked it in the cold water and gently cleaned up Cobb's face. 'It can't be much of a life for you out here,' continued Cobb. 'That man of yours is quite a lot older than you.'

'It's somewhere to live,' she said, giving a shrug.

'Yes,' said Cobb, 'but you offering yourself to any man who comes by . . .'

'As you say, Luke is much older than me,' she said. 'I came out here through one of them agencies which find brides for men out here. I had to get away from where I was pretty damned quick for various reasons. I knew what I was lettin' myself in for in comin' here, so there's no cause to feel sorry for me. In fact everythin' was fine for the first six months then Luke went an' got himself kicked in the balls by a mule. Unfortunately it made him lose all interest in sex. So, to satisfy me – I mean I am a normal woman in that respect – an' to earn a few dollars, we hit upon the idea of me becomin' a prostitute. That was no great hardship on my part, that's what I was back East. Anyhow, we don't get all that many folk passin' through, maybe one or two a week, so I ain't exactly overworked.'

'Well, I guess it's your life,' said Cobb. 'All I've gained from this little encounter is a bloody nose and I still don't know who this Mr Smith is, if that is his name.'

'That's what he calls himself,' said the woman. Cobb looked at her sharply.

'Oh, I've seen him before,' continued the woman. 'Last time was about two weeks ago 'cepting that this time he was headin' towards Wentworth.'

'Did he . . . did you. . . ?' faltered Cobb.

'Sure,' she said in a matter-of-fact way. 'Well, if you can call it that. All he did was make me strip naked an' look at me. Nothin' else, he just looked, didn't even want to touch me. It was very strange. He did pay me two dollars though an' as far as I'm concerned any man can just look at me for two dollars a time.'

'That's exactly what he did with a prostitute in Wentworth,' said Cobb.

'Maybe a mule kicked him in the balls too,' she said with a laugh. 'Somethin' like just wantin' to look at a woman's body might seem strange to a man like you, but when you've been workin' in this business for a while there's not much surprises you an' provided they pay it don't matter that much what they do.'

'I've led a very sheltered life,' said Cobb with a broad grin. He took the wet rag from her and held it to his nose for a while and then looked at it. 'It looks like the bleeding has almost stopped,' he said. 'Thanks for your trouble, I'll be all right now. I suppose I'll have to catch the others up, Silas said they'd wait for me about half a mile away.'

'And you'll have to admit that a man half your size got the better of you,' she said, laughing. 'They'll probably laugh at you.'

'What they think doesn't bother me at all,' said Cobb. 'Still, I suppose I have learned something from all this, so it hasn't been a complete waste of time, even if it has been painful.'

'Such as?' she asked.

'To make sure that my opponent is aware of the rules,' he said with a derisive laugh. 'I must also remember that it does not pay to be a gentleman out here.' He soaked the rag again and walked away holding it to his nose. He gave the woman a brief wave but there were no words of farewell.

The half-mile which Silas was supposed to have travelled proved to be closer to a mile and certainly seemed like even further in the relentless heat of the day. He met Luke Mostyn, who had taken his place on the wagon, making his way back to the trading post. Both men passed each other with nothing more than disinterested looks. The only thing Cobb almost regretted, apart from Smith getting the better of him, was that persuading Luke Mostyn to take his place had cost him two dollars.

'What happened to you?' asked Silas when Cobb eventually reached the wagon which was in the shade of one of the few large trees.

'Let's just say that Smith is a very resourceful man,' he replied. 'I've got a broken nose to testify to that fact.'

'So you didn't find out who he really is or what he wants from us?' said Branagan. 'I hope you killed him if nothin' else.'

'Sorry,' said Cobb. 'It completely slipped my mind. I expect he'll still be following us.'

'Well, there ain't nothin' we can do about it now,' said Silas. 'Come on, let's go, I want to reach a water-hole I know of before it gets dark. Don't worry, Major, I won't say it's your imagination this time. I think we'll be all right though, he had his chance last night an' didn't do nothin', so I don't suppose he'll try anythin' tonight, at least I'll be surprised if he does.'

'I wish I had your confidence,' said Cobb.

The waterhole was reached shortly before sunset; a large, clear pool surrounded by trees. Cobb could not help but think that it was an ideal place for Smith to ambush them, but, like Silas, he had the feeling that nothing would happen. It seemed to him that whatever Smith did want, he was not ready just yet.

The day had been hot and Cobb felt very dirty and the water looked very inviting. He stripped off and threw himself into it, very surprised to discover just how cold it was. His companions looked on with some amusement but none of them was tempted to join him and Silas had made it plain that he would not release their chains even if they did.

Silas cooked a meal consisting of the same unidentifiable dried meat and beans they had eaten the previous night and once again the men were ordered to sit around a tree and the ends of the chain padlocked together.

Reasonably certain that Smith was close by, Cobb decided that he would take the opportunity to scout round. By that time it was dark and thick, ominous clouds had started to develop. Directly overhead however, it was still clear and there was an almost full moon which made things quite easy to see.

After almost an hour of searching, Cobb reluctantly came to the conclusion that Smith was either not there or had expected Cobb to search for him. His feeling was that Smith *was* nearby but had no intention of being found. He eventually returned, somewhat reluctantly, to Silas and the prisoners. It was very noticeable, even in the dark, that in the space of the hour he had been away, the heavy clouds were beginning to close in overhead.

'It could be he decided not to bother,' said Silas. 'Maybe you scared him off. Let's hope so; he's beginnin' to make me nervous as well as them.'

'I don't think he's been scared off,' said Cobb. 'He's apparently been following them for a long time now. I don't think he's going to be scared off too easily. No sir, he's still out there – waiting. Waiting for what though?' He looked up at the dark sky. 'The cloud is getting thicker.'

'Yeh,' agreed Silas. 'Looks to me like there's a storm brewin'. Right time of year for storms too an' when it does decide to rain you'll sure know all about it. We could do without it, we have to cross the Blue

Water River. That's bad enough when there ain't no
rain, but if it gets too full there ain't no way across.'

'Which means what?' asked Cobb.

'Which means that we'll just have to sit it out until
the water level goes down,' replied Silas. 'That could
be anythin' from a couple of days to a week. We'll just
have to hope it ain't rainin' further up country.'

'When should we reach the river?' asked Cobb.

'Providin' there ain't no hold-ups, we ought to be
there by tomorrow night.'

'Hold-ups?' queried Cobb.

'Rain at this time of year has a nasty habit of
causin' land slides,' said Silas. 'There's usually a way
round anythin' like that, but it'll slow us up. Just
occasionally it means that we have to turn back an'
find another way.'

'And do you think that's likely?'

'Won't know until we get there,' replied Silas in a
resigned, matter-of-fact way. At that moment it did
start to rain but at first it was only light. 'It looks like
you is all in for a soakin',' Silas said to the prisoners.
'Come on, Major,' he said to Cobb. 'There's a canvas
sheet under the wagon, you can help me fix it. It
should keep most of the rain off.'

Cobb and Silas manhandled the canvas and eventually it was fixed to the top of the wagon and then
anchored, by means of some stout iron stakes, to the
ground. By that time it was raining quite hard. Silas
indicated that Cobb should join him under the
canvas.

'What about them?' asked Cobb, nodding in the
direction of the prisoners.

'What about 'em?' grunted Silas. 'There ain't

enough room under here for all of us. They'll just have to get wet. They won't rust.'

'We can't just leave them out there,' insisted Cobb.

'We'll have to,' growled Silas. 'Remember what you said, *Major*, I'm in charge an' I say they stay out there.'

'Yes, *Sergeant*, you are in command,' said Cobb. 'We could put them under the wagon though.'

'Why this sudden concern about a bunch of no-good outlaws?' asked Silas. 'Gettin' wet ain't nothin' to what'll happen to 'em when they get to prison. In fact it'll seem like a Sunday school party compared to that.' He looked at Cobb for a few moments and then shook his head and laughed. 'OK, *Major*, you win. Let's get 'em under the wagon.'

With obvious reluctance, Silas unfastened the chain and ordered the men under the wagon and then padlocked one end of the chain to one of the wheels. There was not much room but at least they were able to keep reasonably dry. Shortly after that it seemed that the heavens opened up and rain such as Cobb had only ever witnessed once in his life before descended.

'Let's hope this clears up by the mornin',' said Silas. 'It's goin' to make for some darned hard goin' if it don't.'

'We could wait until it passes,' suggested Cobb.

'*Major*,' sighed Silas. 'That could be days or it could be only hours. There just ain't no way of tellin'. No matter what it's like, we have to move on. Now get some sleep, I reckon you need it.'

Cobb settled down, now feeling very tired. The one blessing of the rain, as far as he was concerned,

was that it was the same for Smith and would probably deter any plans he might have had.

FIVE

If it was at all possible, it seemed to be raining even harder the following morning. Lightning could be seen in the surrounding hills, accompanied by loud claps of thunder. Despite the weather and strong objections from Cobb and the prisoners, Silas insisted that they had to move on, claiming that it might be days before the rain eased. Unfortunately, as far as Cobb was concerned, their route appeared to take them directly into the path of the main storm and both he and Silas knew that from that point onwards they would be in open country. Both also knew that open country was not really the safest place to be in such weather. It was quite possible that the lightning would seek them out since they would be the highest points. Silas, however, seemed determined and Cobb decided not to argue.

The body of the foreman had been left out in the rain during the night and the driving rain that morning did not help in hauling the body across the back of Cobb's horse. Both Cobb and Silas donned waterproof clothing – which both carried – but the prisoners had nothing except the clothes they wore. In a perverse way the fact that they were exposed to the rain seemed to please Silas.

'They were beginnin' to smell,' he said. 'This rain will sure clean 'em off a bit. It's probably the first time in weeks water has reached their bodies.'

'And it could give them something like pneumonia,' observed Cobb. 'They could even die from it.'

'Then it'll save the State a problem,' grunted Silas. 'I ain't paid to worry about what happens to 'em. All I have to do is deliver five bodies an' it don't matter much to me if they is dead or alive. At least the body of that foreman won't rot so fast. Have you ever smelled a rottin' corpse, Major? I have an' it ain't very pleasant I can tell you.'

'Many times,' admitted Cobb. 'Too many perhaps. What do you intend doing with him?'

'If it was left to me I'd just dump him out here an' let the buzzards an' coyotes finish him off,' said Silas. 'The trouble is I expect there'll be somebody who'd ask awkward questions. There is always some busybody who seems more concerned about things like that than what happens to the likes of you an' me. So, I suppose we'll just have to take him with us an' let them sort things out.'

Their journey was very slow; the trail, such as it was, was now nothing more than deep and very slippery mud. In a few places the mud reached half-way up the wheels of the wagon and more than once threatened to bog them down completely.

For the most part the horses could cope well enough all the time they were on level ground, but going either uphill or downhill proved very difficult. On the steeper downhill slopes, the danger was that the wagon tended to slip sideways and, on more than one occasion, threatened to tip over. The first serious uphill attempt proved impossible and they were left with no alternative but to order the prisoners out of the wagon and use them to push it.

At first the men were not much of a help; their shackles proved to be a great hindrance and, very reluctantly, Silas agreed to removing the chain joining them and the manacles round their wrists, although he steadfastly refused to remove their leg-irons. Whilst removing the main chain and wrist-manacles did allow them more movement, they were still somewhat hampered by the chain joining the irons on each leg. However, despite the weather and their still restricted movement, he was taking no chances and both he and Cobb, each with rifles at the ready – something which Cobb considered totally unnecessary – stood behind the men as they struggled to push the wagon. Cobb was quite certain that in four hours they had covered little more than one mile.

At the first sign of level ground, Silas ordered the men back inside the wagon, although this time he did not replace the chain. By that time it appeared that the prisoners were too exhausted to even contemplate escape.

They continued in this manner – pushing up the steeper slopes and walking behind the wagon on the downwards slopes – for most of the day. During that time the rain continued relentlessly and it was quite plain that they would not reach Blue Water River. In fact, by Cobb's reckoning, they had not even covered ten miles and it was probably closer to only six.

They had all been so busy during the day that all

thought of Mr Smith had passed from their minds. It
was not until Silas finally admitted defeat and
ordered that the wagon be pulled under a large overhang of rock, that Cobb gave Smith any thought. He
did attempt to look back but visibility was so poor
that it was impossible to see more than about fifty
yards. However, the feeling that Smith was not too far
behind persisted.

The overhang was almost a cave and was just high
enough to allow the wagon under. The rain tended to
drive in at one end but at least it was large enough
and deep enough to keep most of it off them. As ever,
Silas was again taking no chances and immediately
shackled the men together. Again, Cobb considered
this a rather unnecessary precaution since they were
all completely exhausted and were also restricted by
their leg-irons. That apart, there did not appear to be
any place for the men to go if they did escape.

It seemed that the overhang was used by travellers
quite frequently. In one corner they found a pile of
dry wood and brush, obviously placed there by some
thoughtful traveller. There was also a circle of stones
surrounding the remains of many fires and it was not
long before Cobb had a good fire going.

Water was the least of their problems and in a
matter of minutes after leaving the cooking-pot out
in the rain, it had collected enough to enable Silas to
cook the inevitable dried meat and beans. On this
occasion even the prisoners appeared to appreciate
the food.

'You reckon he's still out there?' Clayton Branagan
suddenly asked.

'Smith?' said Cobb. 'Yes, I should think he is. I

can't really see him giving up now, he seems to have come too far to allow a bit of rain to put him off.'

'Bit of rain!' exclaimed Branagan. 'Hell, I've been caught in storms before but never nothin' like this. All I can say is I hope he catches his death of cold or he slips an' drowns himself. He must be completely mad if he's still followin' us in this.'

'Perhaps I should invite him to join us,' said Cobb. 'This does appear to be the only shelter for miles around.' Without waiting for any response from the others, Cobb went to the edge of the overhang and suddenly called out. 'Smith! Can you hear me, Smith?' There was no response, although it would have been difficult to hear anyone over the wind and rain. 'Come and join us, Smith,' Cobb called again. 'We've got dry shelter and a good fire. We might even be able to find you some food. Your friends are very anxious to meet you, they would really like to know why you are following them. For that matter I'd like to know as well.' Again, there did not appear to be any response and Cobb gave up calling.

'Even if he is out there, you didn't really expect him to take you up, did you?' asked Silas.

'I suppose not,' admitted Cobb. 'It was just to let him know that I know he's still out there.'

'He's there all right,' grunted Sam Strong, 'I can almost taste him. It wouldn't be so bad if we knew who the hell he really is an' why he's followin' us. I've been goin' back on everythin' we've done in the past six months but I can't think of anythin' which would tie in with him.'

'I can think of many reasons,' said Cobb. 'You haven't been exactly idle from what I can gather.'

'I guess not,' admitted Strong. 'One bank robbery – but that was after he started followin' us – two stores an' maybe four homesteads. We burned the homesteads to the ground.'

'After first raping and murdering any women, I suppose?' added Cobb.

'We didn't murder any one of 'em,' snarled Clenton Brakespeare. 'We beat up their men a bit but that's all. No, sir, Sam's right, he don't fit in at all. We all saw him yesterday an' we all swear we ain't never seen him in our lives before.'

'Well if he wants you as bad as he appears to,' said Cobb, 'he'll have to act pretty soon. How long do you think it'll take us to reach Denver?' he asked Silas. 'If the rain eases up, that is.'

'We've still got the Blue Water River to cross,' said Silas. 'If it's been rainin' up country then the river will be way too high an' we'll have to wait. If the rain eases off tonight we might – just might – reach the river by this time tomorrow. If we can get across it'll take us the best part of two days after that to reach Denver.'

That night, it was almost impossible to sleep. For most of the night it seemed that the centre of the storm had settled over them. On several occasions lightning struck the ground quite close to them and thunder made the ground shudder. It did ease off close to dawn and, when the sky did brighten a little, the rain had eased to little more than a steady, light trickle. The outlook, however, was that there was still a lot more heavy rain to come.

Silas ordered an immediate start but although the rain had eased considerably, the ground was still little more than a sea of mud. Once again it proved necessary to use the prisoners on the uphill sections and to walk behind on the downhill.

Cobb reckoned that they had covered about five miles when, as they rounded a corner, they discovered their way blocked by a landslide. Unfortunately for them, it was also along one of the narrowest parts of the trail, following a ledge along the side of a deep, narrow gully. To their left there was a wall of rock rising to about 200 feet and, to their right, an almost sheer drop of at least fifty feet. Silas studied the blockage for some time.

'There ain't no way we can cross that,' he eventually declared, stating the obvious as far as Cobb was concerned. 'A man on a horse could probably cope with it, but there's no chance of gettin' the wagon across.'

'I suppose that means we'll have to go back?' said Cobb. 'Do you know of another way round?'

'Don't know of one off hand,' said Silas. 'Still, it looks like we don't have much choice. There was another valley about two miles back, that's about our only chance. First though, we have to get this damned wagon turned round.'

Cobb looked at the narrow trail and shook his head. 'I'd say that means unhitching the horses and manhandling it. It's not much use pushing the wagon back either. From what I remember the track is even narrower further back. We'll have to try and turn it here.'

'That's about it,' agreed Silas. 'OK, Major, you unhitch the horses an' I'll get them out. Come on, you lot,' he barked at the prisoners. 'You've got to

earn your keep again.' Cobb uncoupled the horses
and led them along the narrow space past the wagon
which was dangerously close to the wet and crum-
bling edge. Silas organized the men into manoeu-
vring the wagon.

'Why the hell should we bother?' said Three
Fingers Foley. 'You got us up here, you get us out of
it.'

'That's exactly what I intend to do,' grated Silas.
'Just remember who has the gun round here. If the
bullet don't kill you then you sure as hell wouldn't
stand much chance down there in that water. You'll
be smashed to pieces on the rocks in no time at all.'

'OK,' said Branagan, with a sardonic laugh. 'So
shoot us.'

'That might not be a bad idea, don't tempt me,'
said Silas. 'If I do it'll sure save me a lot of hassle an'
by the time they find your bodies – if they ever bothered to look an' did find what was left of you – the
buzzards will have picked your bones clean. They'll
never know how you died or even who you was for
sure, so I can tell 'em what I like an' nobody will be
able to prove a damned thing. Now who wants to be
first to try me?' He raised his rifle threateningly at
Branagan. 'I think you ought to be first.'

For a few moments Clayton Branagan tried to
outstare the guard but Silas was not going to be the
one to back down first. Cobb was ready to intervene
but eventually Branagan shrugged and laughed deri-
sively.

'You know, Silas,' he said. 'I actually believe you
would do it an' even enjoy doin' it. OK, we'll turn
your wagon if only 'cos it's just about the only chance

we have of gettin' out of here. Come on,' he said to the others. 'You heard what the man said, he wants to go back, an' I wouldn't trust him not to use that gun an' I for one ain't ready to die just yet.'

Turning the wagon proved very difficult. It was very heavy and it took almost half an hour to turn it so that it was eventually across the track. In that position, however, the rear of the wagon was jammed up against the rock face and the front wheels came within an inch of the edge. Not only that, in their efforts, some of the rock at the edge had become loose, some even dropping into the raging torrent of water thundering along the gully. There was no question of anyone standing too close to the edge. At this point, Cobb assumed command and, strangely, Silas did not raise any objection. Whilst Cobb was giving orders, he kept hold of the terrified horses' reins to prevent them making a run for it.

'OK steady now,' Cobb ordered. 'That thing is so damned heavy it could easily dislodge some of the rock at the edge and we could easily lose it. We have to try and lift it round.'

'*We*, Major?' sneered Cornwall Jimmy. 'I didn't see either of you doin' much to get it even this far.'

'Somebody has to see that you are doing it right,' said Cobb. 'As Silas might say, that's why they made me an officer. Now, you three men on this side get your backs against the wagon, your hands under the side and lift when I give the order. Silas, you and the other two face the wagon, get your hands under the side and you lift as well. When I say "lift" you all lift and move this way.' He allowed them to get into position, checked that they were ready and then gave the order to lift.

The wagon was very heavy and hardly moved off the ground as the men heaved. However, it did move a couple of inches sideways on the wet surface. Encouraged by even this small amount of movement Cobb ordered the procedure to be repeated. After about ten further attempts, the wagon was eventually in position facing down the very slight slope.

During this time, although Cobb had hardly noticed, the black clouds had closed in and the rain had started to come down more heavily. Suddenly the area was lit up brightly as a bolt of lightning crashed into the rocks above them, accompanied by a deafening clap of thunder.

The horses, including Cobb's own, panicked and Cobb himself was dragged along as they tried to escape. One of the draught horses suddenly reared in panic, splayed its front legs in the air for a brief moment and then brought them down. Unfortunately it struck the ground very close to the edge of the gully. The rock suddenly gave way and the horse plunged into the gully, almost dragging Cobb with it, but he let go of the reins just in time.

He managed to bring the other two terrified animals to a halt and looked back. He was just in time to see the heavy wagon also being swept over the edge into the gully as though it were made of matchwood as a fresh fall of rock crashed down directly into it. Fortunately all the men were some-how able to leap to one side and avoid the falling rock, although Branagan and Three Fingers Foley were hit by falling rock and suffered a few cuts and bruises but there were no broken bones.

Cobb managed to tether the two remaining horses to a piece of brush growing out of the side of the rock and then he ran back to the others. For some time all seven of them stared down at the now shattered remains of the wagon. The horse, plainly dead, was being dragged along by the roaring water. Three of the prisoners were on his side of the new landslide and Silas and the other two on the other side. There was about ten yards separating them.

'At least there was nobody in it,' he shouted above the noise of wind and rain. 'I suppose this means we walk from here on. I can't say that I am looking forward to it but we do not have much alternative.'

'Unless you know how to fly,' said Branagan, sarcastically.

'I'm working on it,' replied Cobb. 'OK, you three get yourselves across, I'll bring the horses over.' The men did not argue and gingerly picked their way across the landslide, hampered by their leg-irons but they made it without too much difficulty. By the time Cobb had brought the two horses up, all three were safely on the opposite side.

At first the already terrified horses refused to even set foot on the loose scree and there was no question of Cobb taking the two over together. He tethered the draught horse to a large rock and then tried to persuade his own horse to cross. Eventually, after much coaxing and some pushing and pulling, the horse was persuaded to venture on to the scree. It had not gone more than two yards when the loose rock suddenly gave way and the horse slipped, almost dragging Cobb with it. Somehow, the horse regained its footing but stubbornly refused to move.

In the horse's struggles, the body of the foreman had slipped to one side and the shift in weight meant that the horse was in imminent danger of crashing into the gully. Cobb made a decision. He pulled out a knife and cut the rope securing the body. The body crashed down into the gully and immediately the horse, freed of the weight, surged forward to stand, shivering with fright, on the solid ground.

'There wasn't much else I could do,' he explained to Silas. 'It was a case of lose both or save the horse and I think we need a horse far more than we need a dead body.'

'Too damned right,' said Silas. 'If I had my way this lot would join him as well. Both me an' Tom had a feelin' about this trip an' it looks like we was right. This is the first time I've ever had anythin' like this happen to me. First I lose my partner an' now I lose the wagon. I'm all for shootin' this lot, it'd make things a lot easier.'

'But you won't,' said Cobb.

'No, I guess not,' sighed Silas. 'I was just thinkin' out loud, that's all.'

'Well I suppose I'd better get back and bring the other horse over. We are going to need it,' said Cobb. 'It looks like it's quietened down a bit.' He made his way back across the scree but, although the horse appeared reasonably quiet, it stubbornly refused to even set foot on the loose rock.

'Use your waterproof as a blindfold,' suggested Branagan. 'If it can't see where it's goin' it won't be scared. It's an old trick I learned when I was a kid.'

'That's a good idea,' agreed Cobb. 'I don't know why I didn't think of it.' He stripped off his waterproof, slipped it over the animal's head and then secured it. Almost immediately he was able to lead the animal across the scree without too much trouble. 'Now we've got to go through all that again,' he said, pointing at the original landslide. 'I'll take this one across before I remove the blindfold. Silas, you and the others go ahead.' Ten minutes later, everyone, including the horses, was safely on the other side.

'If we're goin' to walk, how about takin' these leg-irons off?' said Branagan. 'You can't expect us to walk anywhere with these on. I don't think any of us is about to make a break for it an' you have the guns.'

'Son,' sighed Silas, pointing at the shattered wagon. 'I wish I could oblige. If one of you wants to climb down there an' search for the key I'll take 'em off.'

'Hell!' oathed Branagan. 'OK, there is another way, shoot the damned things off.'

Silas examined his rifle and shook his head. 'I got me six rounds, that's all. All my spare ammunition went down with the wagon. Anyhow, look at the thickness of them chains. A bullet ain't goin' to make no impression at all.'

Cobb bent down and examined the chains. 'He's right,' he said. 'You could shoot at those all day and hardly scratch them.'

'Didn't I hear you make some remark to the sheriff in Wentworth about you bein' able to open that safe of his in ten minutes,' said Sam Strong. 'If you is that good these shouldn't present much of a problem.'

'Normally they wouldn't,' said Cobb. 'The trouble

is I need tools and tools are the one thing I don't have. Even if I could find something it would still take time. These irons weren't made to be easy to take off.'

'Another thing,' said Silas. 'We don't have the time. We need to get out of this place. There could be another landslide any time and next time it might take us all with it. Come on, let's go!'

The men grumbled loudly but did not actively protest. Cobb led the way along the narrow ledge, leading the two horses. The prisoners followed with Silas bringing up the rear, clutching his rifle. Fortunately the ledge was solid rock and although wet and slippery in parts, there was no mud to impede their progress.

Cobb reasoned that it was about two hours before they reached open ground. Shortly after that they came upon an old, abandoned, stone-built cabin, which was largely intact. Even though Silas tried to insist that they make as much headway as possible while it was still daylight, Cobb and the prisoners steadfastly refused, claiming that they were too exhausted.

Cobb made a quick search of the cabin, discovered some dry timbers and some ancient kindling wood and soon had a good fire going. The horses too were brought into the cabin and tethered at one end of it. Then all, except Silas, found themselves a dry patch and almost immediately dropped off to sleep – Cobb included. Nobody seemed all that bothered about food – or the lack of it.

The last thing Cobb remembered was the sight of

Silas standing at the doorway, rifle in hand as if expecting trouble.

SIX

Nobody had the slightest idea what time it was and Cobb's pocket-watch had stopped at some time during the night. The only thing that was certain was that it had ceased raining and the sun was high in the sky, although not yet at its highest point. That told Cobb that it was somewhere between ten o'clock and midday and that they had all slept on. Cobb himself had to admit to feeling much better for having done so. However, he was very surprised that Silas had allowed such a thing to happen.

'I suppose you must have been tired as well, Silas,' he called. There was no reply. He looked around but there was no sign of the guard. 'Silas!' he called out, grabbing his rifle and dashing outside. 'Silas, where the hell are you?' There was neither sight nor sound of him.

Cobb ran to the top of a small rise and looked about but there was nothing to be seen except coarse grass, a small lake about fifty yards away and the undulating land rising steadily all around to meet surrounding mountains. There were several small clumps of trees and a few large rocks, but no sign of

Silas. A short time later, Clayton Branagan joined him.

'It looks like he's gone an' got himself lost,' said Branagan. 'Easy done out here an' an old man like him won't last too long, it gets mighty cold at night. Why don't you go look for him, Major? With a bit of luck you might get lost too.'

'And leave you to the mercy of Mr Smith?' sneered Cobb. 'No sir, I am an officer, remember, and a good officer never deserts his men.'

'We won't tell nobody,' said Branagan with a laugh.

Suddenly, the relative silence was shattered by the sound of a gunshot not too far away. Cobb immediately ran towards where he thought the sound originated and flattened himself behind a large rock, where he found himself at the top of a small hollow. He cautiously peered over the rock and gave a sigh of relief when he saw Silas standing over the carcass of what appeared to be either a sheep or a goat.

'What the hell are you playing at, Silas?' shouted Cobb, coming from behind the rock. 'I thought Smith was about.'

'I ain't playin' at nothin', Major,' replied Silas. 'I just shot us some food. Now you're here you can help me gut an' skin it.'

'What is it?' asked Cobb as he approached.

'A sheep what's been left to run wild,' said Silas. 'This must have been a sheep ranch once an' they didn't take all their stock when they left. I caught sight of four or five of 'em earlier on while you was all still asleep. I figured we needed food so I let you all sleep on while I tracked 'em down. Come on, you've got a knife, I haven't. Have you ever butchered an animal before?'

'I've shot a couple but never had to butcher any,' admitted Cobb.

'No, I don't suppose you have,' replied Silas. 'That's the kind of job officers leave to enlisted men. Now's your time to learn. I'll tell you what to do.'

'What about the prisoners?' asked Cobb. 'One of us ought to be there to make sure they don't try to escape.'

'They ain't goin' far,' said Silas with a wry laugh. 'There just ain't nowhere to go an' with them shackles on they won't travel too fast.'

'There's two horses back there, remember,' said Cobb.

'*Major*,' sneered Silas, 'have you ever tried to ride a horse when you're wearin' leg-irons? I don't think they could even mount up an' they sure couldn't sit astride one. Anyhow, it's one good reason for keepin' them shackles on 'em. Don't you worry about them, they'll still be there when we've finished this little job.'

Cobb was not entirely convinced but he had to admit that Silas did have a point. He drew his knife and went towards the dead sheep. It was plain that Silas was quite enjoying giving orders and that he had no intention of helping. Under his instruction, Cobb set to gutting and skinning the animal.

He had seen animals butchered before and it had always looked quite easy when done by someone who knew what he was doing. However, it proved to be a lot harder than he had expected, especially the actual skinning. Not only did it prove harder, it also took a lot longer than expected. Surprisingly, as far as he was concerned, his knife seemed to become blunt very quickly and he had to sharpen it several times on a small, smooth rock.

It was at least half an hour before skin and guts were removed. That still left the job of the actual butchering, which again proved far more difficult than he had imagined. Eventually the animal was fully butchered. The head, skin and guts were left where they were and already Cobb could see two buzzards slowly circling overhead waiting to descend on the remains.

Silas made sure that Cobb carried most of the meat and very quickly Cobb's clothing was thick with blood. Added to that, flies had suddenly appeared from nowhere and, after a very short time, he did not even attempt to fend them off.

'I think we ought to stay here and get this lot cooked,' he said to a smiling guard who seemed to be enjoying the situation.

'Whatever you say, Major,' replied Silas. 'Yeh, you got a point, cookin' it is the best way to preserve it.' Suddenly there was another shot, this time from the direction of the cabin.

'Smith!' yelled Cobb, dropping his load of meat. 'It has to be, they don't have a gun.' He raced off towards the cabin and, as he approached, Branagan and Foley appeared 'What the hell happened?' demanded Cobb.

'Smith!' gasped Branagan, confirming what Cobb knew. 'He shot Cornwall Jimmy.'

'Is he dead?' demanded Cobb.

'Dunno,' said Foley. 'Jimmy was lookin' for somethin' to get these shackles off with round the back of the cabin. I looked out an' saw Smith sittin' on his horse. He shot Jimmy. I didn't hang about for him to shoot me.'

'Where's Smith now?'

'He just rode off,' said Branagan. 'He took one shot at Jimmy an' then rode off.'

'He rode off knowing that one shot was all he had time for,' said Cobb. 'Keep an eye open; I'll go and see if Jimmy is still alive.'

Jimmy was still alive although bleeding profusely from a wound in his shoulder. Cobb helped him to his feet and almost carried him back into the cabin where he examined the wound. By that time Silas had joined them, laden down with the butchered meat which he appeared to be more concerned about than the condition of Cornwall Jimmy. He dumped the meat and bent over to examine Jimmy's shoulder. He sighed and shook his head, but did not appear unduly concerned.

'Looks like his shoulder joint is shattered,' said Silas in a matter-of-fact manner. 'There ain't nothin' we can do about it 'cept strap him up. The only problem is that we don't have anythin' to strap him up with.'

'Then we'll have to use part of his shirt,' said Cobb. 'It certainly looks a mess,' he agreed. 'I've seen wounds like this before and unless we can get him to a doctor pretty damned quick, I don't give much for his chances. Out here, especially now that the rain has stopped, this heat will soon turn it bad ways.'

'You mean gangrene,' winced Jimmy. 'So find me a doctor!'

'OK, Major,' said Branagan with a wry laugh. 'You're the officer, or so you keep tellin' us, you find him a doctor. Officers are supposed to know all about these things.'

'I don't even know for certain which state we're in,' said Cobb. 'How the hell do you expect me to know where there's a doctor? As far as I'm concerned there could be one a couple of miles away or it might be a couple of hundred miles.'

'More like a couple of hundred,' said Silas. 'The nearest big town is Denver but there might be some homesteads between here an' there. Maybe they can do somethin' for him.'

'Get him strapped up,' ordered Cobb. 'I'm going out to see if I can find Smith. I want to know exactly what he is up to and why.'

'He's got his mind set on killin' us, that's what he's up to,' said Branagan. 'I ain't bothered what the hell happens to you or Silas, Major, but I sure am bothered about what happens to me.'

'Me too,' hissed Sam Strong. 'As long as we've got these damned leg-irons on we're sittin' targets. You have to find a way of gettin' them off, Major.'

'Yeh,' agreed Brakespeare. 'You reckoned you could open that safe easy enough, then these should be even easier. Don't give me no bullshit about needin' tools either.'

'OK, OK,' said Cobb. 'I'll see what I can do. Somebody find me a thin piece of iron or something.'

'There's some old tools round the back,' winced Cornwall Jimmy. 'That's what I was lookin' for when Smith shot me.'

'Silas,' ordered Cobb. 'You keep me covered while I look. If you see him, shoot him.'

'It ain't me he wants,' muttered the guard. 'Why the hell should I risk my neck for no-good scum like these?'

'Because he's hardly likely to leave you and me alive even if he does succeed in killing them,' said Cobb. 'He won't want to leave any witnesses.'

'OK,' muttered Silas again. 'Maybe you're right. I ain't such a brilliant shot though.'

'Then give me the rifle,' said Branagan. 'I can hit a fly on a piece of shit at fifty paces.'

'Then again, I ain't that bad,' said Silas. 'I don't want to end up a fly on a piece of shit for you to aim at. Anyhow, I ain't so sure that takin' them irons off is such a good idea. I say we leave 'em on.'

'You're in charge, Silas,' said Cobb. 'OK, for now they stay on. I'm still going out there to see if I can find him though. You can keep a watch out.'

Silas positioned himself by a window as Cobb slipped out of the door. There was a small mound about twenty yards away at the rear of the cabin from where Smith had apparently shot Jimmy. Cobb had not really expected any opposition and the mound was reached safely enough.

He was not too surprised when there was no sign of Smith. For a few minutes he studied the surrounding country, trying to work out any possible hiding-places. There were remarkably few and certainly no more than three places where a horse could be hidden. There were, of course, a few hollows such as the one where Silas had killed the sheep, a few clumps of trees, but nothing obvious. There were no trees or thick brush within about fifty yards although there were a few single, tall pines which left only the thickness of their trunks to hide behind. He was quite certain that Smith was not behind any of them. It was almost as if Smith had simply disappeared.

'Smith!' called Cobb. 'Where are you, Smith?' As before, there was no reply. 'You didn't kill him,' continued Cobb. 'You smashed his shoulder up pretty bad, that's all. He needs a doctor. What do you want, Smith?'

'Don't turn round!' a voice suddenly said behind Cobb. 'Stay just where you are, don't turn round, just listen, I don't want to kill you or the guard, but I will if I have to.' Obediently, Cobb did not turn round, at the same time raising his rifle away from his body to indicate that he was not about to use it. 'First of all, my name is not Smith, but it's one I've got used to and it'll do for now,' continued Smith. 'Secondly I've got no quarrel with either you or the guard. You've got two horses so I suggest that you ride away from here while you can. That way you'll never know what happens to those dirty outlaws.'

'I suppose you must want them pretty bad,' said Cobb. 'What did they do to you and why didn't you do something before now?'

'I want them and I'm going to have them,' Smith rasped. 'Just for the record and the fact that I think you deserve an explanation, I'll tell you.' Cobb made to turn round but a shot thudded into the ground by his feet, obviously intended as a warning. 'I said don't turn round,' said Smith. 'Nine months ago I couldn't have done something like that, aimed at the ground by your feet and hit it so close. In fact I hardly knew one end of a gun from another. I've put a lot of practice in since then just for this moment. I haven't really been ready up till now. Nine months ago those five men robbed my store. They all raped my wife – who was heavily pregnant with our first child – in front of me. Then they nailed me – yes, nailed me through my hands and feet – to the side of the house and used me as a target. I don't know how many bullets I took but I do know that one of them took away my manhood. The doctor said it was a miracle that I survived but I know the only reason was so that I could avenge the death of my wife and unborn daughter. I don't really know what they did to her, but she miscarried and died and my daughter died along with her. This is the first real chance I have had to kill them.'

'They are being transported to prison,' said Cobb. 'The law has them now. They will pay for what they did.'

'There isn't a prison bad enough nor a sentence long enoiugh to punish them,' snarled Smith. 'Take my advice, you and the guard get out of here while you can and leave them to me. I can promise you that they will really suffer for what they did.'

'You will be a hunted man,' said Cobb. 'A court would probably find that you had good reason but the law must be allowed to take its course. If you kill me and Silas you will be no better than them and you will be hunted like any other outlaw. Is that what you want?'

'Once they are dead, I don't care what happens to me,' said Smith. 'I'm not a proper man any more, my wife is dead, what the hell have I got to live for?'

'On a purely mercenary note,' said Cobb. 'I'm

being paid one hundred dollars to get these men safely to prison. I need that money.'

Smith laughed. 'Major,' he said, using the title for the first time. 'Yes, I heard in Wentworth about you being an army officer. They robbed a bank not long ago, I was there when it happened. I was also there when they hid the money. Eight thousand dollars, not the ten thousand the bank claim was taken. I have that money right here with me. You and the guard agree to ride out and it's yours. I don't have any need for it.'

'No deal,' said Cobb. 'I'm going back to the cabin and then we're all going to start walking. Just remember this, I'm a very good shot and at the first opportunity I have, I shall shoot you.'

'First you have to find me,' said Smith. 'Think about what I said, Major. You could leave here a rich man. If you don't, I can't say what will happen. The choice is yours and you just remember that it's not just your life, there's the old man to consider.'

Cobb had the distinct feeling that Smith was no longer behind him. Nevertheless, he turned with extreme caution. It was almost as if Smith had been spirited away. Despite the limited amount of cover, there was no sign of him. After a brief study of the area, Cobb returned to the cabin.

'You found him then,' said Branagan. 'We heard the shot and saw you talkin' to somebody but we couldn't hear what was said.'

'He found me,' corrected Cobb. 'I still don't know what his real name is, but at least I now know why he wants you so bad. I can't say that I blame him either. In his position I might do exactly the same thing.'

'So what did we do to him?' sneered Sam Strong.

'Nailed him to a wall and used him for target practice,' said Cobb. 'You also raped his wife and killed her and her unborn child. For most men simply raping their wives would be reason enough.'

'Nailed him ... hell, that ain't possible,' said Branagan. 'That feller was dead when we left him, I'm certain of that. I know, I checked on him myself an' he wasn't breathin' at all.'

'His wife was still alive as well,' said Brakespeare. 'We might've done a lot of bad things but we ain't never yet killed any women.'

'Then he must be a ghost,' said Cobb. 'At least that would explain how he managed to just disappear into thin air.'

'It don't do to joke about things like that,' said Foley. 'I ain't sure if I believe in ghosts or not but I was brought up in a God-fearin' family who believed in the devil.'

'Well, being brought up with a strict religious background doesn't appear to have worked in your case,' said Cobb. 'Oh, there was one more thing; he claims to have the money you stole from the bank. He says he saw where you hid it and then helped himself.'

'That would explain why Jack Grover came after us,' said Branagan.

'I assume Jack Grover was the foreman,' said Cobb. 'Smith tried to strike a deal with me and I have to admit that it is a very tempting offer, eight thousand dollars is a lot of money. That's the amount he says was stolen. It looks like you were right about it not being ten thousand as the bank claimed. He says he'll give me the money providing Silas and I ride out of here and leave you.'

'Now that's the kind of deal I like the sound of,' said Silas. 'Four thousand apiece. That'd sure keep me in a manner I would like for the rest of my life. I don't know about you, Major.'

'It would certainly go a long way to making life very comfortable,' said Cobb. 'The pity is, I refused it.'

'I guessed as much,' sighed Silas.

'An' all I can say is that you must be completely mad,' said Three Fingers Foley. 'If that had been me I'd've taken the money an' got the hell out of here. Mind, I am kinda glad you didn't.'

'I might yet change my mind,' said Cobb. 'It is a very tempting offer and I'm sure Silas wouldn't say anything for half of it. The point is we are all sitting targets and unless we can stop him I don't give much for our chances.'

'Then I suggest you get these leg-irons off us,' said Branagan. 'Get these irons off an' let us have one of your guns. Me an' Sam are the best shots an' we ain't afraid to kill when we have to. Since Silas don't seem to like the idea of killin' nobody 'ceptin' us, an extra gun would be very useful.'

'You not being afraid to kill is what bothers me,' said Cobb. 'OK, I'll see if I can get the irons off but it's no deal with the gun. I have enough of a problem with Smith and I don't want to chance one of you killing me and Silas and taking the other guns. After all, you have nothing to lose.'

'That's right,' sneered Foley. 'We sure don't have nothin' to lose.'

'What about this meat?' asked Silas. 'Do you intend startin' off now?'

'You're in charge, Silas,' said Cobb. 'But I think we should remain here for the night and start at first light tomorrow. It'll give me time to get those leg-irons off and for you to cook the meat.'

'It looks like I've just lost command, *Major*,' muttered Silas. 'I reckon you probably know best how to handle things from here on. I still don't like the idea of takin' them irons off though.'

'We need to make up time, *Sergeant*,' said Cobb. 'I have to admit that I too would prefer not to release them but it will allow us to travel faster. Now, just in case he's still out there ready to shoot, cover me from that window while I go and see if I can find anything to remove those irons.'

Cobb too was ready to shoot if necessary, but he found the tools at the rear of the cabin without being shot at. Most of the tools appeared to be related to agriculture with a few strange-looking implements which, he assumed, were to do with sheep and sheep farming. All were far too big for the purpose he had in mind, but eventually he discovered what looked like an iron comb with teeth just about the right length and thickness. Using one of the other tools he managed to break off several of the rusting teeth.

He had just broken off the teeth when he had the feeling that he was being watched and looked up to see Smith, astride his horse, about a hundred yards away. For a few moments both men stared at each other but neither attempted to shoot. Eventually Smith rode slowly away and disappeared from view and Cobb did not see where he went.

'He's still out there,' said Cobb when he returned to the cabin. 'I thought he might try to kill me.'

'Yeh, we saw him,' said Brakespeare. 'Now if one of us had had a rifle we might've been able to take him out. That Winchester of yours should be accurate at that distance.'

'And would it have stopped there?' asked Cobb. 'I think not.' Brakespeare simply laughed. 'OK, let's see if I can get those irons off,' continued Cobb. 'Branagan, you sit over here, you can have the pleasure of being the first.'

The removal of the irons proved quite easy and in a very short time all five outlaws were freed and rubbing their ankles where the manacles had been. Cobb was quite surprised at how red-raw their ankles were, despite the irons having been over their trousers.

'Man, you don't know how good that feels,' sighed Branagan. 'At least I can move without trippin' over myself.'

'Just remember that I can quite easily put them back on again,' said Cobb. 'At the first hint of trouble from any one of you, I shall.'

'You've got the gun, Major,' said Branagan. 'I guess that gives you the advantage.'

'I still don't like it,' muttered Silas. 'You won't have to put them on again. At the first sign of trouble I'll shoot all of you.'

'Yeh, Silas,' said Foley. 'I reckon you would as well.'

'You'd better believe it,' Silas muttered again. 'Now, one of you get that fire goin', there's a load of meat here what needs cookin'.'

'I'll turn the horses out,' said Cobb. 'They need to eat as well. Don't worry, I'll hobble them.'

'Smith might shoot them,' said Sam Strong. 'In his position, I know I would.'

'Then perhaps it's as well he isn't you,' said Cobb. 'I don't think he will. He's interested in you, not a couple of horses.'

He led the horses out of the cabin and, as he applied the hobbles, Cobb once again had the feeling of being watched and once again he saw Smith about a hundred yards away. He was tempted to try and shoot, but felt that even though his Winchester did have such a range, he could not be certain of even hitting his target. He gave Smith a brief wave and Smith responded by briefly raising his rifle and aiming at Cobb, but he did not shoot.

Cobb felt that this was simply Smith's way of letting him know that he held the upper hand, a fact of which Cobb was all too aware. He was not looking forward to the following day when they would be in open country. At least the cabin did provide them with some sort of security, but they could not stay beyond that day.

There was an old water-butt outside the cabin and Cobb stripped off and gave his blood-soaked clothes a good washing, then dried them in front of the fire.

That night, mainly to show the outlaws that he was still in command and much to the relief of Silas, Cobb replaced the leg-irons. The other reason was that he did not want the men trying to overpower Silas and himself during the night. He also brought the horses back inside the cabin just in case Smith should attempt to take them during the night.

'Don't worry,' he said to the prisoners. 'I'll take those irons off again in the morning. Now get yourselves a good rest, we've got a long walk ahead of us.'

SEVEN

The following morning, after an uneventful night, Cobb once again removed the leg-irons and they started on their way. The leg-irons and the cooked meat were loaded on to the draught horse, secured by some rope they had discovered in the cabin. It was a fine, dry morning, although there was a hint of worse weather to come as ominous, dark clouds gathered on the mountain tops ahead of them.

At first there was no sign of Smith but, about half an hour into their journey, Branagan suddenly pointed to a small ridge about 200 yards to their right. It seemed that Smith was now making no attempt to hide his presence, although he did appear wary enough to keep at a safe distance out of rifle range. For the remainder of the morning, Smith maintained a presence, never more than 200 yards away. The fact that he did not attempt to do anything, far from making any of them feel any easier, seemed to unnerve the outlaws in particular.

'Why don't he do somethin'?' growled Sam Strong. 'What the hell is he waitin' for, he could pick us off any time he likes?'

'Yeh,' agreed Clenton Brakespeare. 'He's actin' just like a cat playin' with a mouse an' I don't like bein' the mouse.'

'Just keep on walking,' ordered Cobb. 'As long as he keeps his distance we have nothing to worry about. Silas,' he called to the guard who was in the lead with the horses. 'How long do you think it will be before we reach the river?'

'I ain't got the faintest idea,' replied Silas. 'I don't even know where we are an' I've lost all track of time.'

'I thought you knew where we were,' piped up Branagan.

'Well I don't,' muttered Silas. 'I'm just as lost as any of you. I reckon we is headin' in the right direction, that's about all. That don't mean much though, not at the rate we're travellin'. It might be another couple of days yet.'

'An' maybe more,' muttered Branagan. 'Even if we get across the river it's still a hell of a long way.'

'Yeh,' agreed Silas, 'but at least there's a couple of small towns. Maybe we can hire some horses.'

'Allus providin' Smith lets us get that far,' said Branagan. 'Is there nowhere in between? Jimmy needs a doctor.'

'Nowhere that I know of,' said Silas.

'My damned shoulder is killin' me,' moaned Cornwall Jimmy. 'Can't I ride for a while?'

'You don't walk on your shoulder,' snarled Silas. 'As for killin' you, just hurry up an' die for all I care. You walk, just like the rest of us.'

At about midday, having made steady, if rather slow progess, Cobb ordered a rest alongside a small stream and amongst a small group of trees which offered very welcome shade from the sun. The clouds which had been threatening further rain seemed to have dispersed and, apart from a few clouds still in the mountains, the sky was clear.

Their halt among the trees was the first time that morning that they had lost sight of Smith but they all knew he was close by, waiting for them to carry on. Cobb examined Cornwall Jimmy's shoulder and was satisfied that it did not look any worse than it had earlier that morning. Although inflamed, it did not appear that infection was setting in.

The noticeable absence of Smith actually made Cobb feel rather uneasy. At least when he could see him he knew that nothing would happen. He took a brief walk to the top of a small hill, but there was no sign of him. Far from making Cobb feel any better, it made him think that Smith was indeed very close by and possibly planning something. They rested for the better part of an hour before Cobb ordered them forward again.

Almost as soon as they left the comparative safety of the trees, Smith suddenly let it be known that he was still there.

A single shot echoed around and Clenton Brakespeare suddenly crashed to the ground. Immediately they all flattened themselves in the coarse grass, Cobb and Silas with their rifles at the ready.

'Clenton!' called Branagan. 'Are you all right?'

'I think I'm dyin',' moaned Brakespeare. 'I've been hit in the gut. I need help pretty damned fast.'

'You hear that, Major?' called Branagan. 'What the

hell are you goin' to do about it? Are you just goin' to let him pick us off one by one, makin' sure we die slowly?'

'Right now there is not a lot I can do,' replied Cobb. 'Did anyone see where the shot came from?' There was silence from everyone. 'Neither did I,' confessed Cobb. 'Smith!' he called out. 'Where the hell are you? Brakespeare's just taken a bullet in his gut, he needs help. I'm going to see what I can do for him, Smith. If you want to shoot me as well there's not a lot I can do to stop you, but I can't leave Brakespeare, I have to see what I can do for him.' With that he stood up, half expecting to feel a bullet slam into his body, but there was neither sight nor sound of Smith.

The wound, although very messy and plainly very painful if Brakespeare's complaints and moans were anything to go by, did not seem to have hit any vital organs, but the medical knowledge of all of them amounted to very little. With nothing else to use, Cobb ripped Brakespeare's shirt and used it to bandage his stomach.

'Never can tell with that type of injury,' said Silas as he peered almost ghoulishly at the wound. 'Sometimes there ain't much damage but sometimes food an' gut juices leakin' out can cause it go bad ways pretty damned quick.'

'Thanks for nothin',' moaned Brakespeare. 'I think he aimed at my gut deliberately. I think Clay's right, he intends to kill us all real slow, watch us suffer. You have to do somethin', Major.'

'Perhaps you are right,' said Cobb. 'Perhaps he's decided that a quick death is too good for you. I must admit that I can see his point after what you did to him and his wife. Right now though I don't know that I can do anything. It could be that's what he wants. Draw me away so that he can get closer to you. OK, he seems to have done what he wanted for now; let's get going. We've got a lot of walking to do and we can't afford to waste time.'

'You expect me to walk?' moaned Brakespeare.

'As Silas said,' replied Cobb. 'It's your legs and feet which do the walking, not your gut. Now you can either walk or we leave you here and if we do that I don't think you would last very long.'

'You're a hard man, Major,' grated Sam Strong. 'Mind, I shouldn't expect anythin' else from an officer. All the officers I had were real bastards. I guess that's why they were officers. They used to say that senior sergeants never knew who their fathers were, but I reckon all officers never knew their mother either, let alone their fathers.'

Ignoring the protests from Brakespeare and Cornwall Jimmy, Cobb made them walk. Shortly after starting, Smith once again appeared, keeping his usual distance away. His presence actually seemed to spur the two injured men into greater efforts, plainly fearful of being left behind.

For the remainder of that day, Smith appeared quite content to simply follow their slow progress. At about five o'clock they came upon another clump of trees alongside a waterhole and Cobb ordered that they remain there for the night. He once again examined the wounds of both men and was reasonably satisfied the exertions of the day had not caused any further damage to either man. The only thing he did find slightly worrying was that Cornwall Jimmy's shoulder appeared more swollen than it had.

The heat of the day might not have had much effect on the condition of the two injured men, but it had certainly had an effect on the meat carried on the back of the horse. During the day Cobb had not even given the meat a thought and he was somehow very surprised to discover it covered in flies and smelling quite strongly. Not only that, it was obvious that thousands of eggs had been laid in it. The very sight of it was enough to quell any sense of hunger he had.

Silas on the other hand, simply laughed and shook each piece of meat vigorously, seeming to enjoy seeing all the newly laid eggs falling out. When he was satisfied he sliced a piece off and ate it. Very quickly all except Cobb and Clenton Brakespeare were eating the rotten meat, maggot eggs and all. The only reason Brakespeare did not eat any was because of his stomach. Even the thought of food made him feel ill.

'It's all good food, Major,' said Silas with a wry laugh. 'I met a bunch of Indians once who eat things like maggots all the time.'

'I am not an Indian,' grunted Cobb.

'Yes, sir,' continued Silas, laughing even more. 'Maggots, bugs an' worms is all some of them Indians ever eat. One of the nicest tastin' things I ever ate was a sort of Indian cake made up of berries an' grasshoppers.'

'It sounds revolting,' said Cobb. 'Yes, I have heard that there are some people who do eat things like that and not only Indians, but that does not mean I have to like it or to eat it. I'll wait until we find something we can eat. I've seen a few deer tracks, maybe we can kill some fresh meat.'

'Suit yourself, Major,' said Silas. 'It's you what'll go hungry, not me. I wonder what Smith is eatin'?'

'Not fly-blown meat, that's for sure,' said Cobb. 'Don't you worry about me, I'll get by. I once had to go five days without food or water and if necessary I can do so again.'

'I met a drifter once,' said Branagan. 'He reckoned that even out in the driest desert there was always somethin' to eat. All you had to do was know where to look an' know what was good to eat an' what was bad. He even reckoned there was no need to go thirsty either. Only thing I remember was him sayin' that chewin' cactus was as good as a drink of water.'

'Water is one thing there is plenty of,' said Cobb. 'As for anything else, would you know where to start looking?'

'No, sir,' said Branagan, laughing and deliberately taking another piece of meat and picking off a few maggot eggs which he offered to Cobb. 'I like proper food when I can get it, not Indian food or things like lizard or snake. Mind, some of the food they serve up in some eatin'-houses can be pretty foul stuff an' could be almost anythin'. Even maggots taste good compared with some of that food.'

Having tasted some very dubious food in eating-houses, particularly those sometimes found in the more remote parts, Cobb had to agree. He remembered the stew on offer at Luke Mostyn's trading post and shuddered slightly. He picked up a piece of meat and, after wafting away the ever-present flies, studied it for some time. He eventually cast it to one side in disgust, preferring to go hungry.

That night Cobb again applied the shackles to each man, ignoring their protests and assurances that for the moment, at least, they knew they were better off with him and Silas.

He considered going looking for Smith when it became dark, but eventually decided against such a thing. Even if he were able to locate Smith, the darkness would be a considerable handicap and he had to admit that he did seem very resourceful and might well be expecting such a move.

During the night Brakespeare became delirious and, when Cobb examined him, seemed to have developed a fever. It was of no comfort to either man when Silas, almost gleefully it seemed, announced that he was not at all surprised, and questioned whether Brakespeare would survive the night.

Brakespeare did survive the night, but by the morning his condition had definitely deteriorated. His stomach was very swollen around the site of the wound and he was plainly in no fit state to walk. He was helped, complaining loudly, into the saddle of Cobb's horse and once again they set off. Once again it was about half an hour later when they saw Smith keeping his usual distance.

At about midday, they found themselves travelling along a very steep-sided, narrow valley, thickly lined with trees. There was a fast-flowing, narrow river along the bottom, obviously swollen by the recent rains and in many places overflowing on to the track. Although fairly deep in places, it did not present them with any real problems. The track itself was wide enough to have taken the wagon and was, apparently, used quite regularly. On this occasion however, as had been the case all along their journey, there was nobody to be seen.

The narrowness and steepness of the valley meant that Smith was unable to keep his customary watch over them and was, apparently, forced to follow them. This fact gave Cobb an idea.

'Silas,' he said in a low voice just in case the sound might carry. 'I'm going to try and put an end to this Smith following us. I'm going to go up among the trees and wait for him to pass me. You carry on for about another twenty minutes or so and then rest up and wait for me.'

'What if he gets you first?' said Silas. 'How long do we wait?'

'Use your own judgement,' said Cobb. 'If he does manage to get the better of me I'd say it won't be long before you know all about it.'

'That's what worries me,' muttered Silas. 'OK, Major, I guess you know what you're doin'. Good luck.'

Cobb looked behind and, reasonably certain that Smith was not in sight, slipped behind a large rock and then clambered up the steep slope. He eventually found a large tree behind which he hid and from where he could also see the trail. He waited for what seemed an exceptionally long time before he detected movement below.

Smith rode very slowly into view, obviously wary as he studied the slopes either side. Cobb raised his rifle but before he could shoot, Smith had disappeared from his line of sight. He silently cursed himself while on the other hand he was almost grateful. He was not at all certain whether or not he could actually shoot a man in cold blood. Despite having been taught to do so in the army, as an engineer he had never been called upon to do such a thing. In fact he had never used his gun to kill anyone in twenty years of service. He allowed Smith about five minutes before descending back on to the trail.

Cobb followed warily for about ten minutes before he suddenly came upon Smith's horse. This could only mean that Smith had left the trail. Cobb eventually located him among a high group of rocks set between the trail and the river; he was obviously looking down on something. He guessed that the something was Silas and the prisoners resting up as instructed.

Getting close to Smith was something of a problem. Positioned as he was at the top of the rocks and overlooking the trail, he only needed to turn round to be able to see anyone behind him. As far as Cobb could see the only way he would be able to get closer, unseen, was to wade into the fast flowing water, round a large boulder and then climb about fifteen feet.

That approach also presented Cobb with a problem, as he very quickly discovered when, thinking that the water was only about two feet deep, he suddenly found himself plunging into a deep pool.

At first, the force of the water tended to force him under water and back, but somehow he struggled to reach the base of the large boulder where, much to his relief, he managed to gain a foothold. He waited to regain his breath and composure, hope that Smith had not heard the commotion and curse the fact that his rifle had also taken a good soaking.

From experience he knew that water and guns did not mix too well. Sometimes a gun would work normally and on other occasions it simply jammed. Unfortunately there was no way of knowing which of these two possibilities would prevail. All he could do was hope.

After regaining his breath, Cobb swam the short distance round the boulder from where he could climb. If he was correct, this would bring him to within ten feet or so of Smith and from a direction he would least expect. The climb was, of necessity, very slow as he did not want to risk being heard even though the roar of rushing water masked most sounds.

Eventually he reached a small ledge from where he could peer over and see Smith. His next problem was getting into a position from where he could either shoot or have the advantage. As it was, any attempt to shoot from where he was might easily have missed and Smith could have escaped.

Very slowly he eased himself until he was able to stand on a rock and was actually above his quarry. All he had to hope for now was that his gun worked. He slowly raised the rifle and spoke quietly.

'I think I've got the advantage this time, Smith,' he said. 'Drop that gun and raise your hands.'

'And if I don't, Major?' replied Smith in a matter-of-fact manner, almost as if he had been expecting him.

'Then I shoot,' replied Cobb.

'Then maybe you'd better shoot, Major,' replied

Smith. 'I wondered where you were when I didn't see you down there with the others. Well done. I must admit I did think about you coming at me from the river but I dismissed the idea. Well, what are you waiting for? Go ahead and shoot.' He turned slowly to face Cobb, smiled briefly and raised his hands. 'Can you shoot a man who has just given himself up?'

'Damn you, Smith!' growled Cobb. 'Yes, sir, I can.' He felt a knot in his throat. found himself closing his eyes as if this in some way made things easier and squeezed the trigger. The closing of the eyes was something Smith did not miss.

The shot echoed around the narrow valley and the bullet ricocheted off at least two rocks. Cobb opened his eyes to see Smith crouching but with his gun now aimed at Cobb.

'I didn't think you could do it, Major, and there was always the chance that your gun was too wet,' said Smith with a broad grin. 'Try it with your eyes open next time, you might hit your target. I believe I now have the upper hand, Major. Winchesters are wonderful rifles but the one trouble with them is the time it takes to reload and you haven't levered another bullet into the breech.'

'So what are you waiting for?' growled Cobb. 'Kill me and your job of killing the others will be that much easier. That's what you want, isn't it?'

'You have a point,' agreed Smith. 'Rather like you though, I am not a murderer. I don't kill people for the sake of it. It's not you or the guard I want, Major. I am quite happy to let you go, just leave the others. Men like that deserve everything they get.'

'Even if I did,' said Cobb. 'I'd have to tell the

authorities what happened and it is more than likely that they'll send someone out to hunt you down.'

'*Major*,' said Smith, laughing. 'I have one mission in life and I think you know what that is. Once I have achieved that I don't give a damn what happens to me. Here, you said you were escorting them for one hundred dollars . . .' He took a thick, leather wallet from his pocket and tossed it to Cobb. 'There's eight thousand in there, mostly hundred-dollar bills, I don't want it. I'm sure you and Silas can put it to far better use than I can. I'd probably blow it all at some gaming tables or something.' More in surprise than anything else, Cobb caught the wallet. 'Now don't go doing anything stupid like handing it over. I know for a fact that the president of the bank they robbed used the robbery to cover the fact that he had been embezzling from his own bank. I heard him say something about having what they call insurance which covered the loss, so he doesn't want it back.'

'It's still stolen money,' said Cobb.

'Suit yourself,' said Smith with a shrug. 'Can you really afford morals? I know I can't. As far as I'm concerned morals are for people who have no guts to go and get what they want. Nobody's going to thank you for handing it back.'

'You might be right,' admitted Cobb. 'Thanks for the money, I'll keep it and decide later what to do with it. In the meantime though, don't think that it's going to buy me off. It is also a matter of honour. When I agree I am going to do something I feel obliged to carry it through to the best of my ability.'

'Crap, Major!' said Smith, laughing again. 'Where

was the honour when they cashiered you from the army? Yes, I heard about that too.'

'That was personal,' said Cobb. 'OK, so what are you going to do now? It seems to me that you have a choice. You can kill me and make your job that much easier or you can leave me alive. Alive, I intend to make certain that those prisoners reach Denver.'

'I am not a murderer, Major,' said Smith. 'Unless I have to kill you in self-defence I have no intention of killing either you or the guard. I can assure you, however, that when you do reach Denver all you'll have to show for your effort will be five dead bodies.' He laughed again. 'Personally I don't think anyone will he too bothered about that.'

'I intend to hand over five live prisoners,' said Cobb. 'Make your mind up, Smith. Shoot me or let me go.'

Smith laughed and stood to one side, carefully ensuring that his gun was aimed at Cobb. He bowed slightly, obviously mocking Cobb. Cobb jumped down from the rock, levering another bullet into the breech as he did so.

'Don't think I didn't see that, Major,' said Smith. 'I wouldn't try it if I were you. I have become a very good shot, I don't miss from this distance very often.'

'OK, Smith,' said Cobb. 'For the moment you have the upper hand, but it won't always be like this. Not that you are concerned, but there are two injured men down there who need to see a doctor. Do you intend shooting the others but not killing them for the moment? I know what they did to you and your wife, but do you really intend to kill them very slowly?'

'The slower the better,' said Smith. 'I want to see them beg to be finished off. If I could get my hands on them they'd really know what suffering meant.' He held up one of his hands, palm facing Cobb. There was a rough scar and his palm was slightly hollowed 'Do you know what it feels like to be crucified, Major? Well I do and I've spent my time dreaming of all sorts of ways to make them hurt real bad. Now get back to your men, Major. Just remember both you and the guard are safe enough; it's them I want.'

Cobb nodded and scrambled down the rock back on to the trail. For a brief moment he toyed with the idea of taking Smith's horse, even killing it, but he realized that would achieve very little. He made his way towards where Silas had called a halt.

'What the hell's been goin' on up there?' demanded Branagan. 'We heard the shot an' didn't know if it was you or Smith.'

'It was neither of us,' admitted Cobb. 'He got the better of me back at Mostyn's trading post and I am afraid to say that he just got the better of me now, but at least I am still alive.'

'How long for?' asked Silas.

'He didn't say,' replied Cobb. 'OK, let's get going, we still have a few hours of daylight left.'

Silas nodded at Clenton Brakespeare who was lying on the ground. 'He hasn't,' he said. 'He died about five minutes ago.'

Cobb bent down and confirmed that Brakespeare was dead. 'Too bad,' he said. 'I suppose we'll have to take him along. Come on, get him over the horse and just remember, it might have been any one of you. For your own sakes, keep an eye open for Smith. He said he intends to make sure you all suffer.'

'And you?' asked Branagan.

'And me, and Silas, if he has to,' replied Cobb.

EIGHT

When Cobb eventually called a halt for the day, they were still in the valley. Cobb had roughly reset his pocket-watch and it now indicated a time of six o'clock. Although the sky directly overhead was still fairly light, the steep sides of the valley prevented any direct sunlight from reaching the trail. Not having any idea how much further the valley extended, they took shelter under a large overhang about ten feet above the river.

Once again the others sliced off some rotten meat, picked out a few maggot eggs and even quite a few maggots which had developed, and chewed quite happily. Cobb watched with a mixture of revulsion and fascination as he saw maggots and maggot eggs being eaten. Once again he refused; although hungry, he simply could not bring himself to tackle the now writhing meat and marvelled that the others did not seem at all bothered.

There was no sign of Smith, although all of them knew that he was not very far behind and they tried to persuade Cobb to go back and try to kill him. Cobb, however, having twice tried and twice failed, was not too keen to fail a third time. He knew that failure the next time could well result in Smith changing his mind and killing him.

He had not told anyone about having the wallet and thought it wiser if everyone, including Silas, were kept in ignorance, at least for the time being. Apart from the outlaws, Cobb was not too certain as to what Silas might do. Silas was armed and might just decide to kill them all and make a run for it. It was a lot of money and better men than either he or Silas had been tempted by lesser amounts. He did remember that Silas had only the bullets in his rifle but could not recall how many that was and was simply not prepared to take the chance.

The only thing Cobb did do, much to the annoyance of Branagan, was to stand on the trail and shout down the valley knowing that Smith would be able to hear him. It was not so much that he wanted Smith to know that Clenton Brakespeare was dead, it was more a case of confirming that he *was* still there.

'Brakespeare's dead!' shouted Cobb. 'You hear that, Smith, you've just killed a man. Whatever you like to think, you've just committed a murder.'

'One down, four to go,' came the reply. 'I haven't murdered anyone, I've simply removed a piece of vermin. I saw you tie him across the horse so I already knew. He was the lucky one, he died quickly. Branagan, you just remember. Pretty soon now you'll be begging me to let you die.'

'It's still murder,' shouted Cobb. There was no reply and Cobb decided not to bother any more.

Knowing that Smith was very close and probably

could get within rifle range if he so decided, Cobb discussed with Silas the idea of posting a guard during the night. However, knowing that they could never trust the prisoners with a rifle, they decided that the chances of Smith doing anything in the dark were remote and so gave up on the idea.

That night Cobb did not apply the leg-irons, partly because it was a very tricky business using the metal prong and partly because of his belief that they would not make any attempt to escape. That belief was vindicated, mainly because they were all too tired to even think about it.

As soon as it became light enough to see the valley floor, they were on their way again and, much to their surprise, in less than half an hour came to the end of it and out on to a small plateau. Rough grass stretched as far as they could see ahead of them and up to mountains about three miles away on either side. The river which had flowed down the valley now widened but appeared shallower.

Even more surprising and totally unexpected, they could see a stone-built cabin about a mile ahead of them. It was obvious that the cabin was occupied as a plume of smoke curled from the chimney.

'Perhaps now we can get some decent food,' said Cobb. 'I don't know how friendly people are in these remote places though. I hear tales of shooting first and asking questions later.'

'They're not very keen on strangers,' said Silas. 'I remember this farm from a couple of years back. I can't remember anythin' about who lives there though. Most mountain folk don't like strangers. They believe, with some justification, that travellers only mean trouble. Don't expect them to welcome us with open arms.'

'Well, we can but try,' said Cobb.

The first indication was that the occupants were not friendly. Their approach was greeted by a man and woman each carrying a rifle. Not wishing to push his luck too far, Cobb stopped short, ordered the others to remain where they were and went on alone.

'That's close enough, stranger,' rasped the middle-aged man. 'What do you want?'

'Some food would be very welcome,' replied Cobb. 'As you can see there are six of us and we've been walking a long way. We're heading for Denver.'

'I also see a body across one of your horses,' said the man. 'What happened to him and why are you walkin'? Folk don't walk these mountains 'cos they enjoy it.'

'It's a long story,' said Cobb. 'If you will provide us with food I will explain.'

'You can explain now,' insisted the man, raising his rifle at Cobb.

'Very well,' said Cobb. 'My name is Cobb, they call me Major Cobb because I was once a major in the army. The man leading the horses is a guard from the state penitentiary, his name is Silas. He tells me he was this way a couple of years back, perhaps you remember him.' The man simply stared and said nothing. 'The other four are prisoners and Silas and me are escorting them to prison in Denver.'

'We don't want no outlaws here,' said the woman.

'I can well appreciate that,' said Cobb. 'The thing is we were caught in the storms and the wagon in which the prisoners were being transported was washed away. We were able to save two horses, mine and one of the draught horses, but seven men cannot ride two horses so we were forced to walk.'

'How did the other one die?' demanded the man.

'I'll be perfectly honest with you,' said Cobb. 'We are also being followed by a man who is out to kill the prisoners. He shot him. He also shot one of the others in the shoulder and I would appreciate it if your wife could look at it. I am not a doctor.'

'Neither am I,' said the woman. 'Sounds like a load of trouble to me. We don't want no trouble. Why does this other feller want to kill them?'

'Because they crucified him, nailed him to a barn and shot him to pieces but he survived. They also murdered his wife after raping her. The child she was carrying was also killed.'

'Then I hope he does kill 'em,' grunted the man. 'Major, you say, What unit? I was in the army for a few years.'

'Twenty Third Corps of Engineers,' said Cobb.

'Never heard of 'em,' the man snarled. 'I was in the Fourteenth Cavalry, a corporal. Give me one good reason why I should believe what you say. We do get strangers up here from time to time an' they all spin some yarn or other. Most seem to think that my wife is available as well. Get one thing straight, she ain't.'

'I can assure you that no attempt will be made upon her,' said Cobb. 'Other than my word, the fact that only myself and the guard are armed, and some leg-irons which were on the prisoners but which I removed to make it easier for them to walk, I have no proof. All the papers were washed away with the wagon. We do not want to stay, all we want is some food and we'll be on our way. I am willing to pay for what we eat.'

The two looked at each other for a few moments and eventually the woman nodded and spoke. 'You sound like a man what's had book-learnin', maybe you was a major like you say. OK, I'll see what I can find. It won't be much, mutton stew, but at least it's good, wholesome food. It'll cost you a dollar apiece.'

'I thank you,' said Cobb. 'I'll call them forward.'

'Just one thing,' said the man. 'You say you have leg-irons for the prisoners?' Cobb nodded. 'Then put 'em on before they get fed. I wouldn't trust any of 'em not to try somethin'.'

'I don't think I can,' said Cobb. 'We lost the keys in the wagon. I managed to get them off by picking the locks. Don't worry, both Silas and me will make certain that they don't try anything.'

'An' I'll be keepin' my eye on you,' reminded the man. 'At the first sign of trouble I shoot an' believe me I am very accurate. Don't think my wife can't handle a gun either. She can, I trained her.'

'Fair enough,' agreed Cobb.

'An' this feller what's followin' you,' asked the woman. 'He don't sound too friendly.'

'Ma'am,' said Cobb. 'I can assure you that you will get no trouble from him. He is only intent on killing my prisoners. He has said that he doesn't intend killing either me or Silas. You have nothing to worry about.'

'How far behind?' demanded the man.

'That I do not know,' said Cobb. 'Last night he was only a couple of hundred yards behind, but we haven't seen him this morning. I expect he will be along shortly after we leave.'

'Then maybe I'd better make up some more stew,' said the woman.

Cobb led the men towards the cabin where the man made it clear that none of them, not even Cobb or Silas, would be allowed inside and that he would be standing over them all the time they were there.

'Yeh, I remember you,' said the man to Silas. 'You had another feller with you last time an' you were drivin' a big cage with prisoners in.'

'My partner died of a heart attack back in Wentworth,' said Silas. 'Then we lost the wagon. This was goin' to be our last trip but it's turned out the worst one we ever had. I can't recall how far it is to Blue Water River.'

'Walkin'!' said the man, laughing. 'Two days, maybe even three.'

'Then we'd better say four days,' said Silas. 'Do you know if they've had much rain?'

'You saw for yourselves what it's been like,' said the man. 'I can't see it bein' any different down by the river.'

'Perhaps you know of a place where we can cross?' suggested Cobb. 'You must know this territory better than most.'

'When you do reach the river, follow upstream for about five miles,' said the man. 'It widens out just there an' runs fairly shallow even in the worst rain.'

The woman brought out six bowls of mutton stew but demanded payment before she would hand them over. Cobb found six dollars and she was satisfied, although she did test each one by biting the coins to make sure they were genuine. She said something about having been caught out by counterfeit coins in the past.

The stew was not the best Cobb had ever tasted, in fact it was rather bland, but at least it appeared to be made up of decent meat and vegetables, some of which were unknown to him. However, he was, by then, very hungry and ate the somewhat tasteless offering with relish.

The woman also presented them with mugs of what she claimed was coffee. As far as Cobb was concerned, any relationship to coffee was purely accidental, but at least it was hot. He had heard that in some remote places, and even in some towns, the word 'coffee' was applied to many different beverages which appeared to be made up of local herbs or even grass. This mixture fell, he thought, into the category of dried grass. Silas and the prisoners did not appear to notice.

The woman looked at Cornwall Jimmy's shoulder and announced that there was nothing she could do but that in her opinion he needed to see a doctor as soon as possible. She also said that the nearest doctor was in Denver. Having satisfied their hunger and thirst, Cobb announced that they would be on their way, an announcement which appeared to bring relief to the man and woman.

Sam Strong decided that he wanted to use the privy and nobody really gave the matter a second thought as he disappeared behind the building. What they did not see was Strong dash to the horses, which were at the side of the cabin, pull the body of Clenton Brakespeare off Cobb's horse and immediately leap into the saddle. The first they knew of it was when they heard the horse being ridden away.

It was already too late for anyone to get an accurate shot in, although Cobb, Silas and the man all tried.

Cobb's initial reaction was to run towards the other horse, but he gave up on that idea even before he reached it. He knew that the draught horse would be no match for his horse and he was also concerned that Branagan, Foley and Cornwall Jimmy might also try to escape. More important, he was afraid that they might hurt the man and woman in some way.

'Shit!' oathed Cobb in a very rare outburst. 'I ought to have guessed one of you might try something like that.'

'We ain't got no chance of catchin' him now,' said Silas. 'He can probably make the river in less than a day, if he goes that way. I guess you just lost part of your fee, Major. The deal was for five outlaws.'

Branagan laughed. 'That's just what I was goin' to do,' he said. 'Sam was ahead of me on that one. I hope he makes it.'

'He's only bought himself a bit of time,' said Cobb. 'A man like that only knows one way of life. It won't be long before he either ends up dead or he gets caught. I only hope innocent people don't suffer.'

It was noticeable that both the man and woman stood at the door of the cabin, each with rifles held threateningly as they loaded the body of Clenton Brakespeare across the back of the remaining horse. Cobb ordered his charges forward and he also noticed that the couple remained by their door until they were out of sight.

Cobb had suggested that some food might be provided to help them on their way, but this was refused on the grounds that they needed everything for themselves. It was pointed out that there were a few wild goats in the area but they were very difficult to locate.

The going was quite easy as they followed a well-worn, flat road which at first followed the course of the river. When the river disappeared the ground rose slightly to meet a pass between two mountains. Sillas assured them that from that point onwards it was all downhill and very easy going as far as the Blue Water River. After two hours, it suddenly struck Cobb that they had not seen Smith.

'What the hell happened to him?' he wondered out loud. 'I can't see him giving up now.'

'As far as I'm concerned I'm glad he ain't around,' said Branagan. 'He makes me bloody nervous, I don't mind admittin'. Let's hope somethin's happened to him like he had a fatal accident or somethin'.'

'Anything is possible, I suppose,' said Cobb. 'I must admit that I too am glad he's not watching us.'

'Maybe he went out after Sam,' said Three Fingers Foley, laughing. 'If he does get close to Sam he won't back off like you did.'

'I did not back off,' grunted Cobb. 'I didn't see him ride past us, did any of you? It was pretty flat back there, we would have seen him.'

'I saw a couple of deep gullies,' said Silas. 'It would've been easy for a man on horse to get by unseen. Anyhow, none of us would be expectin' somethin' like that so none of us was lookin'.'

'I suppose not,' agreed Cobb. 'I still don't think it likely though.'

There was no sign of Smith for the remainder of the afternoon nor when they eventually pulled up for the night among a group of trees. There was none of their rotten meat to eat, for which Cobb at least was grateful, and the meal they had had at the cabin had quelled his hunger for the moment. They missed their chance to kill a deer when Silas startled one as he was collecting wood for the fire. A search of the small copse did not turn up any other deer.

Nights on the high, open plateaux were often very cold and this night was no exception; they were more than grateful for the fire. However, tired as he was, Cobb's mind was active, wondering why they had not seen any sign of Smith. Although most welcome, the absence of Smith also bothered him.

The following morning was uneventful and again there was no sign of Smith. By that time Cobb was beginning to believe that he must have met with some sort of accident. If that was the case then he certainly had no intention of going looking for him. He felt the wallet of money in his breast pocket and smiled. Perhaps fate had played into his hands. If Smith had met with an accident he was either dead or would not survive long. If that was the case then there was nobody to say where the money he now possessed came from.

By mid-afternoon the open ground had given way to forest and with forest came the prospect of finding deer or other small mammals they could eat. It was Silas who called a halt.

'I just seen a small deer,' he said. 'Wait here while

I go look. It looked like a young 'un, so where there's young there's other deer nearby.'

By that time feeling hungry and with the prospect of several more days on the road until they reached Denver, Cobb agreed and waited with the prisoners. It was now very important that one of them remain with the prisoners as it would have been all too easy for them to escape into the forest and if that happened they might never be found again.

After about ten minutes there was a single shot and eventually Silas reappeared carrying the carcass of a small deer. Cobb for one was thankful that it was only a small animal since it would be sufficient for them for one meal and they would not have it go rotten on the horse.

'Well done, Silas,' he said. 'Let's find somewhere to rest up and cook it. Keep going, we'll soon find somewhere.'

They did find a very suitable place. It was a clearing with a shallow stream running through and several large trees around the edges under which they could shelter. It was also here that they discovered evidence that Smith was still with them. . . .

At first they all stood and simply stared at the body of Sam Strong; it seemed obvious that he was dead. He was completely naked, his arms stretched between two trees and with what proved to be large nails driven through his wrists and into the trees. His body was covered in blood which was now congealed and alive with flies. Nobody needed any telling as to what had happened.

'Bloody hell!' gulped Branagan. 'The bastard

crucified him an' shot him to pieces.' He stepped forward for a closer look. 'He even shot his balls off.'

'Just like you did to Smith,' reminded Cobb. 'I suppose someone had better check that he is dead. You thought Smith was dead, remember.' All four outlaws drew back, shaking their heads. 'I suppose I'll have to look,' continued Cobb. 'He certainly appears to be dead and for some time as well.'

It did not take Cobb very long to establish that Strong was dead. If his other injuries had not killed him a bullet hole in his chest indicated that that at least had delivered the fatal blow.

'What you goin' to do, Major?' asked Silas. 'As far as I'm concerned he can stay where he is.'

'You said something about delivering five bodies, Silas,' said Cobb. 'So, we deliver five bodies. Come on, we've got to get him down.'

'Smith seems to have learned a thing or two,' grunted Silas. 'He nailed him through his wrists so's the nails wouldn't pull through. The weight of a body nailed through the hands would drag the nails through.'

'You seem to know a lot about such things,' observed Cobb.

'It's somethin' I remember readin' in a book,' said Silas. 'Them nails is in pretty deep, Major, how you goin' to get 'em out? We could do with a claw hammer. Smith must've had one an' some nails.'

'Probably the same nails he was crucified with,' said Cobb. 'You're right, though, but we don't have anything we can use. I suppose we'll just have to pull his wrists off them. Come on, Branagan, you can help me.' Very grudgingly, Branagan did as he was

ordered and he grasped Strong's arm while Cobb
pulled on his hand.

It proved surprisingly difficult to pull Strong's
wrist off the nails and when they eventually
succeeded with the first wrist, there was a distinct
breaking of bone as the nail slid through.

With Silas and Foley holding the body, the operation was repeated on the other wrist, with same difficulty and cracking of bone. Eventually the body was
allowed to drop to the ground and immediately both
Silas and Foley rushed to the stream and threw themselves into it in an effort to rid themselves of the
unwelcome blood.

Cobb straightened the body out and briefly examined it. He counted fourteen separate wounds apart
from the damage to Strong's penis. Cobb had the
distinct feeling that that particular wound had not
been inflicted by a well aimed bullet, but by a knife.
He gagged slightly and looked around for the
dismembered organ but was unable to find it, not
that he really wanted to.

'Well, at least we now know that Smith is still
around,' he said.

'Is that all you have to say, *Major*?' hissed Foley.
'The man must be insane to do somethin' like this.'

'Just as you were when you did it to him?' asked
Cobb. He looked about the clearing. 'There's no sign
of the horse. Either Smith took it or it wandered off.
His clothes are over there, I suppose somebody
ought to try and dress him.'

'What the hell for?' sneered Silas. 'He ain't goin'
to feel the cold no more.'

'For decency's sake if nothing else,' replied Cobb.

'At least we can cover him over for now, it might keep some of the flies off him.'

Cornwall Jimmy went to gather the clothes and found a piece of paper which he studied for a moment before handing it to Cobb.

'My readin' ain't too good, maybe you'd better see what it says.'

Cobb took the paper and read through it. 'All it says is two down, three to go,' he said. 'It also says he isn't too far away.' He looked about the clearing and suddenly called out. 'OK, Smith, we get the message. Just remember that if I do get you in my sights again I won't close my eyes.' There was no response, not that he had expected any. 'Now, we've got us a deer to cook,' he continued. 'Silas, collect some wood.'

'I don't feel like eatin',' muttered Branagan, a sentiment endorsed by Foley and Cornwall Jimmy.

'Then you can go hungry,' said Cobb.

NINE

There was absolutely nothing any of them could do to prevent the ever-present flies swarming around the mutilated body of Sam Strong. The only thing they could do was to put the horse on a long rein and make certain that it was always down wind of them. They took it in turns to lead the horse.

The only one who admitted to having slept reasonably well that night was Silas. Silas was also the only one who appeared completely indifferent as to what had happpened. Even though Cobb was also indifferent towards the fate of the prisoners, it had become a matter of pride with him. So far that pride had been severely dented in that he had failed to prevent the killings.

They travelled through the forest for most of the day and it seemed that any thoughts the three remaining outlaws might have had of escaping – and there were numerous opportunities for escape – were put well to the back of their minds. As Clayton Branagan admitted, for the moment there was safety in numbers.

Cornwall Jimmy's shoulder had become very

discoloured and Cobb feared that gangrene was
setting in, he had seen it before, although he did his
best to assure Jimmy that this was not the case. Silas
was not quite so tactful, he declared that Jimmy
might as well kill himself now, since gangrene in the
shoulder was one of the worst places to get the
disease, he was certain to die.

Ambush was possible almost anywhere along the
trail and at first every little movement or sudden
noise had them ducking for cover. However, the
longer they went on without any sound or sign of
Smith, the less nervous they became. Cobb had to
admit to himself that he was surprised that Smith had
not attempted to shoot any of them. The conditions
for ambush were as near perfect as they could ever
be. However, he was quite certain that Smith was very
close to hand.

Shortly after midday, they suddenly came upon
the missing horse standing in a small clearing obviously terrified of something. Cobb guessed that the
animal had bolted from the scene of the earlier
carnage. The reason why the horse was so frightened
suddenly became very obvious as a low growl was
heard nearby.

'Wolves!' announced Silas. 'Looks like we found
your horse just in time.'

'To hell with the horse,' hissed Cornwall Jimmy.
'What about us? I don't want to end up as wolf meat.'

'Since you is goin' to die anyhow,' said Silas with a
sarcastic laugh, 'you might as well serve some useful
purpose. Even wolves have to live somehow an' they
don't mind a bit of rotten meat. They can smell all
this dead meat we're carryin' an' that rotten shoul-

der of yours. The time to get really worried though is when a buzzard comes an' sits on your other shoulder. I know for a fact that buzzards don't care if it's people or other animals they eat. I've seen quite a few bodies what have been picked clean by buzzards.'

'Take no heed of him,' said Branagan. 'I have heard that wolves don't attack people. Mind, I wouldn't like to put it to the test an' buzzards only eat dead meat.'

'That's right,' said Cobb. 'Despite all the stories you might have heard, that's all they are, stories. There have never been any recorded incidents of wolves attacking a man, let alone eating him. Some people say that they sometimes dig up graves but even that has not been proved.'

'That's probably 'cos nobody has ever lived to tell the tale,' muttered Jimmy. 'Even if what you say is true, they still make me bloody nervous.'

Cobb raised his rifle and fired a single shot in the direction of the wolves and immediately several animals could be heard crashing through the undergrowth. 'I hope that makes you feel better,' said Cobb. 'Come on, keep walking. The wolves won't bother us and we still have a long way to go.'

With the second horse now in tow, they continued through the forest for about another four hours. Eventually the trees thinned out and they found themselves on an open plain. The track followed the course of a small river which, they assumed, would feed into the main river, the Blue Water River. At about six o'clock Cobb called a halt for the day among some rocks alongside the river. The two bodies were placed well away from them, downwind, but where they could be seen. The call of a bird overhead made them look up and they saw two buzzards circling.

'They is lookin' for their dinner,' said Silas, laughing.

'Then they'd better look somewhere else,' muttered Cornwall Jimmy, unthinkingly feeling his shoulder. 'I ain't ready to become buzzard meat just yet.'

'So what happened to Smith?' asked Branagan. 'I've had this gut feelin' all day that he's breathin' down my neck.'

'Well we ought to see him from now on,' said Cobb. 'It's open country ahead, there's nowhere he can hide.'

'You said that when we was up at that farm,' said Foley. 'He sure got by us then without bein' seen. For all I know he might be standin' behind that rock over there right now.'

'I doubt it,' replied Cobb. 'Still, if it makes you feel any easier, why don't you go and take a look. I think I can trust you not to try and make a run for it.'

'I might just do that,' muttered Foley. 'I'd feel a whole lot easier if I knew for certain that he wasn't there.'

'And the first you'll know about it is when he shoots you,' said Branagan.

'I'd still like to know,' insisted Foley. 'As far as I'm concerned there's nothin' worse than not knowin' for sure.'

'Then do something about it,' said Silas. 'I'm stayin' right where I am.'

'It's OK for you,' muttered Foley, 'it ain't you he

wants. Why don't you go take a look, Major?'

'If you want to know, you find out,' replied Cobb. 'He'll show himself when he's ready.'

'Damn it, I will,' hissed Foley. 'I'd feel a whole lot safer if I had a gun though.'

'And I'd feel a whole lot safer if you didn't,' said Cobb.

'Just keep me covered,' grunted Foley. 'I'm goin' to take a look.'

Foley marched off towards a large rock about 200 yards to their right. He had almost reached the rock when suddenly there were two rapid shots. Foley crashed to the ground and Cobb found himself running forward. Another shot thudded into the ground close by his feet, bringing him to a halt. He knew that that particular shot had only been a warning and that Smith was more than capable of killing him if he so desired.

'Three down, two to go,' came the voice of Smith. 'Don't force me to take you out as well, Major.'

'I wondered just where you were,' called Cobb. 'I must confess that I did not expect you to be so close behind. I'm going to see if you killed Foley. If you want to kill me, go ahead, I am hardly in a position to do much about it am I?'

'He's dead,' assured Smith. 'Two bullets straight through his head.'

'Very likely,' replied Cobb. 'I'm still going to make certain though.' Without waiting for Smith to say anything, Cobb walked slowly towards the body and bent down to examine it. 'Just like you said,' he called. 'Two holes in his head. That was some real fancy shooting.'

'I've had a lot of time to improve,' said Smith. 'A lot of time and any number of good reasons.'

'At least you killed him cleanly,' said Cobb. 'That's more than can be said of what you did to Sam Strong.'

'Sam Strong deserved everything I did to him,' called Smith. 'He was the bastard who nailed me to the barn and the first one to take my wife. I'm glad I had the chance to give him a taste of his own medicine. The other one I'd really like to get my hands on is Branagan, he was the bastard who suggested nailing me to the wall. OK, Major, you can take him back. I suppose you feel honour bound to deliver five outlaws, even if they are dead outlaws.'

'Five outlaws and one murderer,' said Cobb. 'No matter what you think, killing those men is murder.'

'In your eyes, maybe so,' called Smith. 'Perhaps the law might agree with you as well, but I don't give a damn what you or the law thinks. Five outlaws and one murderer, first you have to catch me or kill me, Major. Do you think you can do that? You've had two chances and failed both times.'

'I shall certainly try,' assured Cobb. 'I don't think I'll fail a third time.'

Cobb dragged the body of Three Fingers Foley back to the camp, where he found the remaining two prisoners and Silas crouching behind whatever cover they could find. Cobb eventually convinced them that for the moment the danger was past, but Branagan and Cornwall Jimmy did not seem entirely convinced, even when they saw Smith, at a safe distance, ride on ahead.

'At least we now know he's ahead of us,' said Silas.

'Not that that's goin' to help you two much. How about a small wager, Major,' he said to Cobb. 'I'll give you odds that these other two are dead by this time tomorrow.'

'And possibly even you,' said Branagan.

'It's you two he wants, not me or the Major,' reminded Silas. 'As far as I'm concerned he can have you as well. I sure ain't goin' to risk my neck tryin' to save you. I'd like to live to retire with my widder-woman.'

'Then I reckon the best thing you both can do is leave us here,' said Branagan. 'That way you'll never know what happens to us.'

'I promised to deliver five prisoners,' said Cobb. 'When I make a promise I don't go back on my word. I'll deliver the five of you even if you are all dead.'

'Yeh, I think you would too,' sneered Branagan.

The buzzards circling overhead were obviously becoming bolder and both birds suddenly dropped down alongside the three bodies. Cobb shot at them, forcing them to take to the air again and he immediately ordered that the bodies be brought closer, where they could be protected.

'There's not only the buzzards,' he said, pointing to the opposite side of the river. 'There's a couple of coyotes over there as well. I know coyotes and foxes will eat anything, including dead people. Silas, one of us will have to keep watch all night to make sure they don't sneak in.'

'You can forget me,' said Silas. 'I don't give a damn if they get eaten or not.'

'OK, if you don't mind having to deliver half-eaten corpses, neither do I,' said Cobb.

'OK, OK, Major,' sighed Silas. 'You take first watch, you've got the timepiece. Wake me up at about two o'clock.'

The coyotes maintained a presence all night, but they were unable to get at the bodies although both Cobb and Silas were kept reasonably busy holding them at bay. It seemed that none of them was able to get much sleep and they were on their way as soon as the first rays of light appeared.

From that point onwards a constant watch was kept for any sign of Smith and, although there were one or two places where he might have been able to shoot any one of them, there was no sign of him.

For the most part the country was open and flat and there was a sigh of relief from all of them when Silas suddenly pointed ahead.

'Blue Water River!' he announced. 'Should be there in another hour.'

'About five miles upstream the man at that farm said,' said Branagan. 'Maybe we can get across before then. I won't feel safe until we're on the other side.'

'Maybe Smith's already across,' said Silas. 'Thing is, if he is goin' to do anythin' else he has to do it soon.'

'We'll cross as soon as we can,' said Cobb. 'Can you all swim?'

'I ain't never had cause to learn,' admitted Silas.

'Me neither,' groaned Cornwall Jimmy. 'Even if I could, I don't think I'd get far with this damned shoulder.'

'Then it looks as though we'll just have to find this shallow part and hope it's not too deep with the water running as high as it appears to be,' said Cobb.

'In the meantime, keep your eyes peeled for Smith. Silas is right, time is running out for him. You've been this way before, Silas, where did you cross?'

'There used to be a ferry across,' said Silas. 'Last I heard though it had got washed away in a flood an' they never bothered to replace it. We'll soon find out though, it should be about a mile after we join the river.'

'Let's hope that they've replaced it,' said Cobb.

It was exactly an hour later when they reached the banks of the river. Cobb looked at the swollen waters and wondered how it had ever acquired the name of Blue Water River. It was obvious that the recent rains had caused the river to flood and, although the level had plainly dropped, it was still very high and appeared to be of a very muddy consistency. There was no question of attempting a crossing at that point.

They slowly continued upstream and about half an hour later came to where Silas claimed the ferry had been. There was the remains of a shack and evidence, mainly submerged, of a landing stage but no sign of a ferry on either side of the river. At that point the river was about 400 yards wide. They continued upstream for about another two hours and, although the banks were lined with trees and thick bushes, there was no sign of Smith.

They heard the sound of rapids before they actually reached them. The river widened to what was at least half a mile and was broken into numerous channels, each cascading over rocks and waterfalls and creating many small islands. The recent rains had obviously made all the channels a lot deeper than normal, but even so it seemed that there were plenty of places where they could cross. Cobb carefully selected what he thought was the best route and led the others forward. The mainly smooth rocks were very slippery and all, including the horses, found gaining a foothold difficult. After reaching the first of the islands, Cobb revised his plan.

It had been his intention to make most of the crossing over a large expanse of smooth rock and through one or two narrow channels. However, with the rock proving more slippery than expected, he opted to head through slightly deeper water from island to island.

They were about half-way across, between two islands, when Cornwall Jimmy suddenly gave a shout and for a moment clung to a rock. Before any of them could get to him, he slipped under water and disappeared from view. There was nothing anyone could do or attempt to do as Jimmy's apparently lifeless body briefly reappeared but was then swept away. He was eventually caught in the quieter water amongst some rocks where he lay, apparently lifeless. He was too far away for anyone to be able to reach him.

Cobb, Silas, Branagan and the two horses with the three bodies eventually made the safety of the island. Cobb looked for Cornwall Jimmy's body but could not see it at first. He eventually caught a glimpse of it being washed further downstream and towards the far bank. He resolved to go in search of it once they were across.

The remainder of the crossing took them about two hours. More than once they were all in danger of being washed away but somehow they eventually made the crossing. During that time all thought of Smith had disappeared from their minds. Cobb did think about him once they were on the far bank, but by that time they were all far too exhausted to do anything but lie in the grass. The horses too were shivering from their ordeal. It seemed that sleep overtook them all.

Cobb awoke with a start and found himself staring up at a night sky. Immediately he grabbed at his rifle and looked about. To his relief he saw that both Silas and Branagan were still there. He allowed them to sleep on.

When Silas and Branagan eventually woke up, Cobb had managed, by vigorously rubbing sticks together, to get a fire going. Being wet and cold, all three huddled round the fire.

'What about Jimmy?' Branagan asked eventually. 'Do we look for his body?'

'We?' queried Cobb. 'I wouldn't have thought you would have been bothered what happened to him.'

'I ain't all bad,' said Branagan. 'Me an' Jimmy have been together ever since he walked out on his ma more'n six years ago. He's almost like a younger brother to me. I'd like to know he had a decent burial at least.'

'We'll look for him in the morning,' promised Cobb.

'Thinkin' about your money?' sneered Branagan. 'OK, I guess that's as good a reason as any.'

The night passed without incident and as soon as it was light enough to see, they set off downstream, searching the muddy banks. After more than an hour without any sign of Jimmy's body, Cobb was about to call a halt when Silas suddenly pointed at a small sandbank about ten yards out.

'That looks like him,' he said. 'That looks like an arm stickin' up.'

Both Cobb and Branagan peered closely and agreed that it did indeed look like an arm. It appeared that the bulk of the body had been submerged in mud left behind by the now rapidly falling river.

'Can you swim?' Cobb asked Branagan. The prisoner nodded. 'Then we'll both swim out there. The water's fairly calm, it shouldn't be too difficult.' Both men stripped down to their longjohns and waded into the water, both very surprised at just how cold it was.

They reached the sandbank without difficulty and discovered that it was indeed the body of Cornwall Jimmy. Using only their bare hands, it was about twenty minutes before they had recovered the body from the mud. They both swam back to the bank with the body between them.

'At least Smith didn't have the satisfaction of killin' him,' said Branagan as they dressed. 'Maybe it was as well, I don't think he would've survived much longer with that shoulder of his in the state it was.'

'That leaves just you,' gloated Silas. 'You don't think he's goin' to give up now do you? From now on you'd better keep your eyes peeled. If he's goin' to make a move he has to do it soon. There's a settlement not far away. Nothin' much, just a few houses an' farms. As far as I know they don't have no lawman.'

'It's better than nothing,' said Cobb. 'Maybe we

can buy or hire another couple of horses. How far to Denver?'

'If we get horses? Another day at most,' said Silas. 'There's an army outpost between there an' Denver. We could hand this lot over to them.'

'We'll see,' said Cobb. 'OK, put Jimmy across my horse and let's get out of here. I haven't seen any sign of Smith yet, but I'll guarantee he's around somewhere.'

Whilst Cobb readjusted the bodies of the other three outlaws on the other horse, Branagan pushed the body of Cornwall Jimmy across Cobb's horse. He glanced round, saw that both Cobb and Silas were occupied and suddenly leapt into the saddle, pushing off the body as he did so. Before either Cobb or Silas could react, he was racing away. Cobb tried to shoot but his rifle had taken a soaking when they had crossed the river and the hammer simply clicked harmlessly. Silas did not even attempt to shoot. Branagan was very quickly out of range.

'Damn!' oathed Cobb. 'I should've expected something like that.'

'That you should,' agreed Silas. 'It was about the last chance he had.'

'Why didn't you shoot?' demanded Cobb.

In reply, Silas laughed, raised his rifle, and squeezed the trigger. The hammer fell harmlessly. 'Same reason as yours didn't work,' he said. 'I tried it while you two were swimmin' out for the body. It didn't work then so I knew it wouldn't work this time. It's full of mud.'

'Well we have no chance of catching him now,'

said Cobb. 'Come on, let's get to this settlement you mentioned.'

'Maybe we won't catch him,' said Silas, 'but I wouldn't say he's got away. Smith is still around somewhere.'

'But where?' asked Cobb, looking about and at the fleeing Branagan, apparently heading in the opposite direction to the settlement. 'He might not even know he's managed to escape.'

'I reckon he'll know,' said Silas. 'He seems to have known everythin' else so far so I can't see him lettin' Branagan escape now.'

'You could be right,' said Cobb. 'In a way, I hope Smith doesn't get him. If he doesn't, Branagan will get caught somewhere.'

'What about Smith?' asked Silas. 'You did say you were goin' to take him in as well. It looks like you've missed your chance.'

'That's what I like about you, Silas,' said Cobb. 'You have the ability to state the obvious.'

'And it's obvious to me we've got to get to this settlement,' said Silas. 'If nothin' else we can get somethin' to eat. I'm starvin'.' Cobb grunted something uncomplimentary, took the reins of the horse and strode on.

They reached the settlement at mid-afternoon and were quickly surrounded by about a dozen curious onlookers, some prodding at the bodies across the horse and making obvious, Silas-like, comments about them being dead.

'You're Silas ain't you?' said an older man. 'I seen you before. Ain't you a guard with the prison?'

'Was,' grunted Silas. 'I just resigned. These are

what is left of some prisoners we was escortin' Four dead an' one escaped.'

'An' him?' asked the man, nodding at Cobb.

'Meet Major Cobb,' said Silas, sarcastically. 'Major Cobb, late of the Corps of Engineers, now tryin' to make a livin' escortin' prisoners.'

'For the first and last time,' replied Cobb. 'I can think of easier ways to earn a living. Is there any chance of some food?' he asked the man. 'We haven't had anything to eat for at least two days.'

'Food costs money,' grunted the man. 'For a dollar apiece I reckon my woman can rustle up some grub.'

'Some folk are very obliging in these parts,' said Cobb. 'I think you would even charge a man who was dying of thirst for water.'

'Nope,' replied the man in a matter-of-fact way. 'Water's free. Drink as much as you want. Food'll still cost you one dollar apiece.'

'OK, OK,' sighed Cobb. 'I know when I'm beaten. One dollar apiece it is and for that I don't expect something which even a pig wouldn't eat. I want good, wholesome food.'

'Only the best,' said the man. 'My place is over there. I'll even throw in some fodder for your horse.' He called to an elderly woman. 'Food for the gentlemen,' he said. 'This one's very particular, but then what else would you expect from an army officer.'

'I've got ham or I've got stew,' replied the woman.

'I'll take the ham,' replied Cobb, very wary of exactly what the stew might consist of. 'I fancy ham, eggs and flapjacks.'

'Ready in about half an hour,' replied the woman. 'Just one thing. Them bodies don't look or smell too wholesome. You keep 'em well away from my place.'

'You can cover 'em over with a canvas sheet,' said the man. 'There's one in the barn just inside the door. If'n you want to stay the night, you'll have to sleep in the barn as well.'

'The barn will do fine,' said Cobb. 'Thank you.'

After stabling the horse and covering the bodies, Cobb and Silas were allowed inside the house where, for the first time in many days, Cobb glanced at himself in a mirror.

'After we've eaten, would you mind lending me a razor,' he said. 'I knew I wanted a shave but I didn't realize I was quite so bad. I'd appreciate a bath as well if that is at all possible.'

'A razor I got,' replied the man. 'If'n you want a bath, there's a tub of water round the back.'

'No hot water?' he queried.

'A bath in hot water?' asked the woman, plainly surprised. 'I puts hot water on for bathin' at Christmas an' it sure ain't Christmas yet.'

'No ma'am,' agreed Cobb. 'I should've realized.'

TEN

A breakfast of what the woman claimed to be bacon, eggs and fried potatoes cost them another dollar each, for which Cobb duly paid. There was no question that the eggs and fried potato were exactly as claimed, but the true identity of the bacon was very much open to question. There were four rashers each consisting mainly of fat. Nevertheless, it was most welcome.

Cobb also managed to negotiate the hire of three mules. The hire of horses appeared completely out of the question, since there were, it was claimed, only two horses in the whole settlement. The hire of saddles for their horse and one of the mules also met with a firm refusal, which meant that both of them would have to ride bareback. The mules proved to be rather bony animals so Cobb gave way to age and allowed Silas to ride the horse.

The cost of hiring the mules was finally agreed at three dollars each animal, having started at ten dollars and been haggled down. The man told Cobb to leave the mules at a place called Stacey's Livery in Denver from where they would be collected, subject

to Cobb agreeing to pay the livery charge for one
week. By mid-morning Cobb, Silas and two of the
mules with two bodies each across them, finally left
the settlement.

Both men had spent most of the previous evening
cleaning and oiling their guns and both seemed satisfied that they were now in good working order. The
man even found some bullets for Silas's rifle, for
which, out of the goodness of his heart the man
claimed, there was no charge. Cobb almost made the
comment that the cost of the food they had
consumed more than compensated for the bullets,
but he refrained from saying anything. The true
reason was probably that nobody in the settlement
had a gun which was the right calibre for the bullets.

From that point onwards, the going was mainly on
the flat and through open country interspersed with
small sections of woodland. The going might have
been easy, but Cobb had quite forgotten how slow
and uncomfortable mules could be and these particularly bony animals seemed more uncomfortable
than usual. He even questioned whether it might
have been quicker to walk.

By mid-afternoon, when they stopped for a brief
rest, Cobb's legs and thighs felt as though he had
been run over by a wagon. He spent almost all the
half-hour they rested pacing up and down in an
effort to restore some feeling in his legs.

'At this rate it's going to be another three days at
least before we reach Denver,' said Cobb. 'What say
you, Silas?'

'Just about right,' agreed Silas. 'If we'd been able
to get horses we would probably have made it by

tomorrow evenin'. I know mules is mighty uncomfortable to ride,' he continued, 'but then this horse wasn't bred as a ridin' horse. It's too wide across the back to sit comfortably.'

'Oh well, I suppose it is better than walking – just,' said Cobb. 'Come on, we've got another few hours of daylight ahead of us, let's get as far as we can.'

'Do you reckon we've seen the last of Smith an' Branagan?' asked Silas when they were once again on their way.

'Well I don't think Smith is following us any longer,' said Cobb. 'I think he must have seen Branagan make a run for it and went after him.'

'Yes, poor sod,' said Silas. 'I know I don't have much time for folk like Branagan but I almost feel sorry for him. Do you reckon they'll send anyone after Smith?'

'Probably not,' said Cobb. 'They might even say he did them a favour by killing them all. After all, it means less trouble and expense and the man did have good cause to want revenge. I wonder what his real name is? I know it isn't Smith. You said something about there being an army post between that settlement and Denver. Any idea how far?'

'I ain't too sure,' said Silas. 'I ain't used to ridin' this slow. If we don't reach it tonight I reckon we should be there some time in the mornin'.'

They continued largely in silence for the next few hours and were passing through one of the frequent stretches of woodland when Silas, who was a few yards ahead of Cobb, suddenly stopped.

'My God!' he exclaimed. 'I think we just found Branagan.'

Cobb caught up with Silas and both men stared at a body hanging from the branch of a tree. Even at the twenty yards distance they were, there was no mistaking that the now bloated features of the hanged man were those of Clayton Branagan.

Closer examination of the body showed that he had plainly been made to suffer before he died. Whether or not it had been the hanging which had finally killed him was open to question, although Cobb suspected that he had probably been alive. A snort from nearby alerted them to the presence of Cobb's horse.

'I wonder how long he's been hanging?' said Cobb. 'Not too long I suspect, some of that blood looks too fresh. This changes things though,' he continued. 'It means that Smith is still around.'

'Well I reckon he was left hangin' here 'cos Smith knew we'd find him,' said Silas. 'You is right about that blood bein' fresh. I reckon he was on the look-out for us an' hanged him when he knew we were comin'. That means he must be around here some-where, maybe even watchin' us right now.'

'You could be right,' agreed Cobb. He looked about but did not expect Smith to show himself. 'OK, Smith,' he called. 'We've found him. What's your next move?' To his surprise, Smith answered.

'I've achieved what I set out to do, Major,' came the response. 'You and Silas are quite safe. At least now you'll be able to keep your pledge and deliver five prisoners.'

'I would have liked to have delivered five live pris-oners,' said Cobb. 'I also made you a promise that I would hand over one murderer as well – you.'

'First you have to catch me, Major,' replied Smith. 'There's just one thing. If you do try to take me, I won't be able to keep my promise not to shoot you. The choice is yours, Major.'

'One day, Smith, one day,' called Cobb, knowing full well that his chances of catching Smith now were almost zero.

'One day, Major,' replied Smith with a derisory laugh. 'Perhaps even sooner than you think.' The sound of a horse being ridden away told them that Smith had gone.

'And what do you think he meant by that?' asked Cobb.

'Darned if I know,' said Silas. 'I don't mind admittin' he's one man I don't want to meet again.'

'I have the strange feeling that we might just meet up with him again,' said Cobb. 'I'll be ready for him when we do.'

'Just leave me out of it,' said Silas. 'Well, I suppose we'd better cut him down, I've seen a few hangin's in my time an' there's somethin' about them which gives me the jitters. I think it's the way the face swells up.'

'I agree,' said Cobb, drawing his knife. 'I'll climb up there and cut him down.'

With the body on the ground and the rope removed, Cobb looked at his pocket-watch and suggested that they might as well spend the night where they were. Silas did not appear too keen on the idea but reluctantly agreed.

They came upon the army post rather sooner than they had expected. They had started out just as dawn

broke – Cobb once again giving way to age in allow-
ing Silas to ride his horse whilst he rode the other.
They reached it in just over three hours.

As expected, their arrival caused something of a
stir as people crowded round to stare and comment
at the bodies. Cobb noted that roughly half of the
onlookers were Indians, rather sorry-looking Indians
at that.

The post seemed to consist of a small stockade
surrounded by about twenty or thirty houses, a
general store and what proclaimed itself to be a
saloon. The sign over the porch bore the name FORT
GEORGE SALOON AND CASINO, which told Cobb that
the army post was Fort George.

Cobb wondered if any of the crowd had ever seen
a dead body before. Many of them asked the obvious
and stated the obvious about the dead men. Cobb
and Silas ignored all comments and questions.
Eventually an officer from the fort pushed his way
through, briefly lifted the heads of each corpse and
stared at them both.

'You, I know,' said the officer to Silas. 'You're a
guard with the prison. You I don't know,' he said to
Cobb. 'Perhaps you can explain just what the hell's
going on here and who these are and why they are
dead? From the state of them I'd say you've got some
difficult questions to answer.'

'*Were*, Lieutenant,' corrected Cobb. 'They were
prisoners being taken under escort to the state penitentiary in Denver. As you can see, things did not go
exactly according to plan.'

'Then it looks like you *do* have some explaining to
do,' said the lieutenant. 'Bring them into the stock-

ade.' He turned and marched to the fort. Cobb and Silas looked at each other, shrugged and followed.

A soldier indicated that the lieutenant had gone into an office and that Cobb and Silas were to follow. The mules and the horses were hitched to a rail where another soldier stood guard over them.

Cobb and Silas entered the office where the lieutenant was now sitting behind a desk. Cobb had seen the name on the door, *Lieutenant Wilson – Commanding Officer*. Lieutenant Wilson did not look up, but pretended to be absorbed in some papers. Cobb smiled, he had seen this ploy many times by junior officers trying to make themselves appear more important than they really were. He had even done so himself in his early years. Eventually the lieutenant pushed the papers to one side and stared at them.

'Well,' he said. 'I am waiting for an explanation.'

'I reckon the major had better explain,' said Silas.

'Major?' queried the lieutenant and plainly ill at ease. 'Major who?'

'Ex-major,' corrected Cobb. 'Ex-Major Cobb, late of the Twenty Third Corps of Engineers.' He produced an old document which had been in a leather wallet in his saddle-bag and had somehow managed to survive. It was proof that he was, or had been, a major in the 23rd Corps of Engineers.

The lieutenant's attitude underwent a sudden change and he became rather more reverential and immediately ordered two chairs brought in. 'Retired or not, Major,' he said. 'You must appreciate my position. I have to check on any unusual happenings.' Cobb nodded and did not correct the mistaken impression that he was retired. 'I know Silas is employed as a guard; have you taken up that kind of work as well?'

'This is strictly a one off,' said Cobb. 'Those men were arrested in a town called Wentworth. . . .' He went on to explain what happened and about Smith. He conveniently neglected to tell the lieutenant about the $8,000 or how he had come by it, the main reason being that he did not yet want Silas to know.

'So this Smith is close by,' said the lieutenant. 'To be honest I'm not quite certain as to what my duty is in such a matter or even if arresting Smith would be legal. Perhaps you know?'

'I was an engineer, Lieutenant,' reminded Cobb. 'Apart from building a few bridges and some railroad track, I never became involved in civil matters.'

'That's just it, Major,' said the lieutenant. 'I know murder is murder but it's normally dealt with by a sheriff or marshal, unless it concerns only military men. You must know that standing orders state that we, the military, must not become involved in strictly civil matters unless called upon to do so by someone in authority and this sounds to me like a civil matter.'

'Yes, Lieutenant,' said Cobb, 'I am well versed in standing orders. I think that the best thing to be done would be for you to provide us with suitable transport as far as Denver. If we carry on with those mules it'll take us another two days at least and those bodies don't smell too sweet even now.'

'Consider it done, Major,' said the lieutenant. 'As a matter of fact there are three wagons leaving for Denver first thing in the morning. I'll arrange everything. In the meantime I dare say you are both tired, dirty and hungry. You must stay here tonight. I shall arrange a bunk for Silas, you can have the spare room next to mine. It is kept for visiting officers. Unfortunately, as I am the only officer at this fort, we do not have special catering arrangements for officers. I eat exactly the same as the men.'

'It sounds fine,' said Cobb. 'You said something about feeling dirty. The one thing I would really appreciate is a bath. Would that be possible?'

'Give me half an hour,' said the lieutenant. 'If you require a bath, Silas, the men's ablutions are across the yard.'

'It ain't Christmas,' grunted Silas, looking at Cobb and smiling.

'Christmas?' queried the lieutenant. Cobb explained about the woman at the settlement. 'In comparison to some I know, she must be very clean,' said the lieutenant. 'I know at least three men and probably even more women who have never had a bath since the day they were born. I'll show you to your room, Major.'

He called a soldier from an adjoining office and ordered him to escort Silas to the bunkhouse and find him a bunk. Silas made some comment under his breath which Cobb assumed was not very complimentary towards officers and followed the soldier across the yard. The horses, mules and bodies were led away to the far side of the yard.

Later, feeling very much better after his bath and having time on his hands, Cobb decided to sample the delights of the Fort George Saloon and Casino since it was the only place which offered any form of alcoholic drink and entertainment.

Word had obviously spread that he was, or had been, a major and it was noticeable that several soldiers suddenly found that they had more pressing duties to attend to as he walked in. The civilian population also drew back slightly. Cobb ordered a beer and looked about. As ever, the customers of the bar were all white since Indians were not allowed in such places or to drink alcohol.

'We don't often get senior officers in Fort George,' said the bartender. 'Most soldiers, especially officers, seem to think being sent here is some sort of punishment.' He laughed. 'I guess it is too.'

'I must admit that I'm surprised to find the army here,' said Cobb. 'There can't be that much for them to do.'

'Indians,' said the bartender. 'We gets trouble from the Indians from time to time, that's why they're here. We ain't had no bother for a few months now though. All it takes is for a few of the young bucks to get their hands on some whiskey an' they seem to think they can take on the world. I reckon we'll get trouble in the next week or two.'

'By which time I will be long gone,' said Cobb. 'Your sign says this is also a casino. I don't see much evidence of it.'

'The gaming tables open at six o'clock tonight,' said the bartender. 'If you fancy a game of cards, I dare say somebody will oblige. If it's a woman you want, that can be arranged too. You can have your pick, white or Indian. The law turns a blind eye to havin' Indian women in the bars on account of there ain't enough white women in these parts.'

'I'll think about it,' said Cobb.

Cobb did not take much notice when someone entered the bar. His back was towards the door and he was appreciating what proved to be a good glass of beer. It was only when, out of the corner of his eye, he saw several customers suddenly leave their tables, looking very strangely in his direction. He slowly turned to see Smith standing in the middle of the room, legs slightly apart and with his hand hovering over the pistol at his side. For a few moments both men simply stared at each other, although Smith did not seem at all surprised.

'I said we'd meet sooner than you might expect, Major,' said Smith. 'Do you still want to hand me over to the authorities?'

'I think all the killing you've been doing recently has turned your mind,' said Cobb. 'It can't have escaped your notice that this is an army post.'

'It hasn't,' said Smith.

'They also know all about you and I dare say that even now someone is telling Lieutenant Wilson that you are here. You certainly haven't tried to hide your presence.'

'Then we'd better get this over with before anyone gets here,' said Smith.

'Exactly what do you want?' asked Cobb. 'I thought you'd achieved everything you set out to do.'

'Strange as it might seem, Major,' said Smith. 'I am a very religious man. I justified killing those men on the basis of an eye for an eye, as it says in the Good Book.'

'So what?' said Cobb. 'That doesn't explain why you are here now, challenging me.'

'I also firmly believe in the afterlife, in heaven and

hell,' continued Smith. 'I believe the Good Lord selected me as an instrument of His revenge. I have carried out the Lord's work.'

'Get to the point,' said Cobb, wearying of the conversation.

'This is the point,' replied Smith suddenly drawing his gun.

A bullet hit the bar counter close to Cobb and, purely by reflex action, Cobb drew his gun. Another bullet shattered some glasses on the shelf behind Cobb and again, without thinking, Cobb fired.

A strangely peaceful kind of expression suddenly appeared on Smith's face and he slowly crumpled to the floor, blood soaking into his shirt and the gun in his hand dropping harmlessly. Cobb immediately rushed forward and knelt down, taking Smith's head against his knee. He was still alive but only just. He looked up at Cobb and smiled. He seemed strangely satisfied.

'I think you wanted me to kill you,' said Cobb. 'I should have known you could shoot better than that.'

'As I said,' grimaced Smith. 'I am a very religious man, Major. What I did to those outlaws was just retribution. Thanks to you I can now rejoin my wife and daughter.' He smiled again, and a trickle of blood oozed from the corner of his mouth. Cobb glanced up and saw Lieutenant Wilson and several soldiers, all with guns at the ready, staring down at them. 'Unfortunately, Major,' croaked Smith, 'my religion does not allow suicide. To take my own life would have condemned me to everlasting torment in the fires of damnation.'

'So you deliberately made me kill you?' said Cobb.

'It was the only way,' croaked Smith. 'I almost made you do it when you found the body of Branagan, but I needed to be certain. I spent all night reading my Bible and could not find another way. I thank you, Major, but I am not sorry for the trouble I caused you. You were never in danger though. To kill you would have condemned me to hell as a murderer.'

'If you are so religious, what about those prostitutes?' asked Cobb. 'I would have thought consorting with women like that would have been against your beliefs as well.'

'Had I been a whole man, I still would not have touched them,' croaked Smith. 'The Good Book does not prevent a man from looking. They were very like my wife, that's all. By the way, Major, my real name is Newall, James Newall. I'd like you to have that name engraved on my headstone.' His eyes closed and he smiled. 'It is time, they are waiting for me,' he whispered. 'Farewell and thank you, Major, I wish you luck.' There was a long sigh as the breath left his body and his head dropped to one side. He was dead.

'You heard what he said,' said Cobb, looking up at the lieutenant. 'He made me do it. I killed him in self-defence.'

'I heard,' said the lieutenant. 'I don't think anyone will try to accuse you of murder. It's the first time I've ever known a man deliberately get himself shot though. There's no accounting for religious beliefs. I shall have to make a report of course, but I believe it will only be a formality, at least I hope so.

The final decision must be left to Marshal Swinburne at Denver.'

'I appreciate what you say,' said Cobb. 'Do you know, in twenty years in the army, Smith – or Newall as he is really called – is the first man I have ever killed. That must seem strange to you, Lieutenant.'

'Not so strange,' said the lieutenant. 'I've been in the army five years and I haven't killed a man yet, not even an Indian.'

By that time Silas had also joined them and Cobb told him what had happened. Silas simply nodded and made some comment about it probably being the best way.

They left the fort the following morning, Silas electing to ride on one of the wagons and Cobb riding his horse, having given Lieutenant Wilson his word that he would not try to escape.

The wagon train consisted of three civilian supply wagons and two soldiers, who were both plainly ill at ease at having a senior officer in their charge, even if he was, as they were told, retired.

They reached Denver at mid-afternoon the next day and, for a time, Cobb was held by the military, although he was treated with respect and not really considered a prisoner. An hour later he was taken before Marshal Samuel Swinburne who had been given the report written by Lieutenant Wilson.

'I already knew about you being employed to escort the prisoners,' said the marshal. 'This report from Lieutenant Wilson makes it pretty plain that you had no choice but to kill this man Smith – or Newall. What happened to the others was most unfortunate and perhaps it could be argued that you did not carry out your duties to the best of your ability. However, I don't think we need pursue that aspect any further. Consider yourself a free man, Major.'

'Ex-Major,' corrected Cobb. 'I think that you ought to know that I am not entitled to use that rank. I know retired officers are allowed to use their rank but I did not retire. I was cashiered for striking a fellow officer.'

'Thank you for being so honest,' said the marshal. 'As a matter of fact I already knew about that and the circumstances. However, as far as I am concerned it does not change a thing. In my opinion, as an ex officer myself, I consider your punishment very harsh. I believe any other man would have done more or less the same thing under the same circumstances.'

'Thank you, Marshal,' said Cobb. 'There is just one thing. Branagan and his gang were supposed to have robbed a bank. I believe the money was never recovered.'

'And not likely to be,' said the marshal. 'In fact the president of the bank does not appear too keen on having it found. I have my suspicions about that man but without proof there is nothing I can do. Anyway, he claims the loss was covered by something they call insurance, whatever that is, so nobody loses anything. Putting it another way, Major, nobody gives a damn about that money.'

'So if someone was to find it they could keep it?' said Cobb.

'Something like that,' said the marshal, smiling knowingly. 'Were you thinking of looking for it?'

'It was a thought,' said Cobb. 'It's a lot of money and I don't have the benefit of a pension.'

'Then I hope you find it,' replied the sheriff.

Cobb left Denver two days later $4,000 the richer, plus the agreed $100 which was reluctantly paid for his escort duties. The other $4,000 he had given to Silas on the understanding that he was not to say a word to anyone. He did not think the guard would tell anyone since he had as much to lose as Cobb did. Silas immediately resigned his position and as Cobb rode out of town in one direction, Silas rode out in the opposite direction to take up farming with his 'widder-woman'.

Unlike Silas, Cobb had no idea where he was going or what he was going to do. The only thing of which he was certain was never to agree to escort prisoners.